THE DECEIVERS...

"Marv tells me I should make a new will," Dave said.

So that he and Gloria can have fun in Paris in the spring? Sue thought, remembering the conversation she had overheard.

He and Marv had talked it over very carefully, Dave was saying, "And I gave him a free hand..."

Sue drew a deep breath. She longed to tell him: "You poor fool, you blessed, trusting idiot. Can't you see that you're being had by two designing people? A man who pretends to be your loving brother, a woman who pretends to be your loving wife?"

But, she didn't say it...

**PUT PLEASURE IN YOUR READING
Larger type makes the difference
This EASY EYE Edition is set in large, clear, type—at least 30 percent larger than usual. It is printed on scientifically tinted non-glare paper, for better contrast and less eyestrain.**

The Nurse And The Crystal Ball
Florence Stuart

VALENTINE BOOKS
NEW YORK

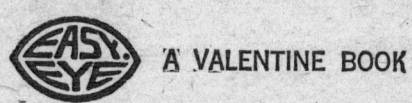 A VALENTINE BOOK

THE NURSE AND THE CRYSTAL BALL

Copyright © 1969 by Arcadia House
All rights reserved
Printed in the U.S.A.

Valentine Books are published by
PRESTIGE BOOKS, INC., 18 EAST 41ST STREET
NEW YORK, N.Y. 10017

Chapter 1

Susan Whittier knew the letter by heart.

She had read it dozens of times since the day she had found it waiting, like a ghost from her past, in the nurses' dormitory back in Maryland.

Now, after three weeks and three thousand miles of driving, she thought of it instantly when she woke up in the La Jolla hotel room.

From where she lay she could see storm clouds gathering in the sky over the Pacific. Hoping this wasn't an ominous sign, she assured herself, as she already had over and over and over, *It was right for me to come.*

How could she have ignored the moving, piteous appeal from the man she had once imagined she loved so dearly? And yet—

Trying to close her mind to the doubts that kept flickering through her thoughts, unbidden, with her mind's eye she read the letter again.

It began: "In all these seven long years, my darling Sue, I have never stopped loving you. Your smiling blue eyes come to me in my dreams. My longing fingers seem to touch the silky sheen of your dark hair. Now the doctors tell me I have only a short time to live. Leukemia, they say."

As always, at the thought of what that meant, she choked up. When she had seen him last, Dave Harding had been the picture of health. And until their last sad meeting when she had told him—had had to tell him—that she must call off their wedding plans, he had been so vital, so filled with the joy of living.

Now it was next to impossible to think of him as a dying man. Nor did she want to see him like that. "If you hadn't come on this wild goose chase," whispered her haunting doubt, "you could have remembered him always as he used to be."

And what good could her coming really do? It could not give him back his health. Nor could she be sure the emotional impact of seeing her again might not do him harm.

But there was the heart-breaking appeal in the letter.

"I keep thinking of the last thing you told me, sweetheart. Short of marriage, you said, you would always be eager to do anything in your power to bring me happiness and peace. It was a kind of promise. So I am daring to write and ask you if that promise still holds. Will you come back to California and serve as my nurse in the little time I have left? It won't be for long. A few months, at most. Maybe only a matter of weeks.

"And to see you once more, to have you near me for whatever time I have left on this earth, would mean the difference between heaven and hell. *Will you come?*"

She had written him that she would come. Refusing to pay attention to the persistent doubts which warned she was letting her pity, her tender heart, overrule her better judgment, she had asked for indefinite leave from the hospital where she had been put in charge of a ward for problem children.

She had traded in her dilapidated old Volkswagen for a new model and set out, with Dave's letter in her handbag, and doubts and uncertainty crowding her mind.

At times the doubts were so strong it was almost as if whispering voices were warning her. "You may be walking into trouble."

Nonsense.

She slid her legs over the bed and reached for the phone to order coffee sent up. Some strong, hot coffee was what she needed. That would clear her head, put an end to silly premonitions and warnings.

Peg Talmadge, her roommate, was the one who told fortunes and believed in such nonsense. Susan certainly didn't.

Laughing to herself, she got up and opened her traveling bag to get out the plastic case containing her toilet articles. Tucked away under a stack of nylons, her fingers discovered the glass ball.

"That crazy girl," Sue murmured. It was Peg's crystal ball. She must have put it in the bag when Sue wasn't looking. Peg's idea of a joke.

Dropping the ball back in her bag, Sue went to

take a quick shower. Back in the bedroom, she put on dark flannel slacks and a blue sweater. Dave had always liked her in this precise shade of blue. He said that it matched her fabulous eyes.

Poor Dave.

He had always seemed to see in her a beauty that wasn't really there. She had never been anything more than a reasonably attractive girl with a lot of wavy dark hair and deep blue eyes. But Dave had seen her with the eyes of love.

The coffee came.

Sue filled a cup, took a sip, then carried it out to the narrow balcony overlooking the ocean. Angry little waves were smashing against the beach directly below.

As she stood there sipping the coffee, she heard a voice quite clearly. "Hello there! Mind telling me where you got those fabulous blue eyes?"

It was the voice of memory, reminding her that this was the very stretch of beach where she had first met Dave Harding.

Tall, blond, and handsome, he had strolled over to her where she lay sun-bathing. She had not fallen in love with him at first sight, although he had with her. Or so he had always claimed.

Actually, she realized later, she never had fallen in love with the man himself. A seventeen-year-old girl had been in love with love. That was what it really amounted to.

And of course he was so darned good-looking and charming. And he could afford to take her to all the posh, expensive night spots. And he was such a marvelous dancer.

All in all, it added up to the perfect romance a girl dreams of finding on the beach in the summer.

It was some little time before she learned that Dave Harding was an extremely wealthy young man and six years older than herself. Nor did he know that she was just out of high school, and the daughter of a widowed mother who lived on a small pension and had had to scrape together the pennies and dimes to rent a tacky little beach cottage for a few weeks.

But in the long run, none of that had made any difference. After her mother's sudden death that fall, Dave had insisted on an immediate marriage.

"Somebody has to take care of you, darling," he had said. "And I love you."

Martha, Dave's mother, had taken Sue to her heart and said the same thing. "You're as dear to me as an own daughter, Sue." And she started making plans for a pretty little wedding in the drawing room at Hillcrest.

For days Sue lived in a dream—until the night when she went down to the beach again with another man. And that other man took her in his arms. And her dream of forever and ever love with Dave was forever blasted.

That other man was Dave's half-brother. Never again, after that one time, had she known his dark gaze on her face, or felt his lips, eager and urgent on her own. They had had only that one moment in time to know the wonder of love—and the bitter taste of parting.

But it had been a moment which had changed the whole course of Sue's life.

There was a far-away look in her eyes as she drained the coffee cup and thought: I wonder if I'll see Marv when I get to Hillcrest?

Just putting it into words filled her with a deep disgust at herself. You idiot, she fumed inwardly, are you still mooning over Marv Crowell?

Stamping back into the bedroom, she put the coffee cup back on the tray. As she hurriedly got her things together, she kept up a running battle of words with herself.

She had done right to tell Dave she was too young, too unsure of her own feelings, to rush into a hasty marriage. It had been the right and kind thing never to let him know that his half-brother had had anything to do with her decision.

What was more, it had been the most sensible thing she had ever done to pull up stakes, leave California, take up nurse's training, and build a new life for herself far, far away.

But if she was still nourishing a secret longing to see Marv again, that was wrong, wrong, wrong.

When she was ready to leave, she took a last glance in the mirror. The words she said aloud to her reflection were alive with something close to self-loathing.

"If you haven't forgotten that man by now, there's something seriously wrong with you.

Maybe your head needs a psychiatric overhaul. So once on a moonlit night there was a man on a beach. He kissed you, and you went slightly out of your mind. That's understandable. That can happen to any girl. But do you plan to go on dreaming about him for the rest of time?

"And what about now? Are you afraid to see him again? Afraid you'll discover he's forgotten your existence? Is that the reason you're half afraid to return to Hillcrest? *Is that what all your doubts and uncertainty are about?*"

She scowled at the mirror as if it were her own worst enemy. "Why don't you grow up, Sue?"

Once she was in her car, driving the last few miles which would take her to Hillcrest, she began to feel better about everything. She was looking forward to seeing Martha, who would, she knew, take her into her arms and cry a few tears. Martha was the kind of loving, demonstrative person who cried easily, especially when she was happy.

As Susan turned into the long drive leading up to the white colonial house on the hill, everything looked much the same as it had the last time she had seen it. It was hard to believe it had been seven long years since she had last driven with Dave between the double line of tall eucalyptus trees which now swayed and danced in the stormy wind.

She was still a little distance from the big house when she braked the car in front of the guest cottage.

Almost as if on cue, the cottage door opened.

The man who came out was tall, with Indian black hair and fiercely dark eyes set in a square-jawed face that Sue had tried hard to forget—but never had.

"Hello, Marv," she said. "Remember me?"

Her smile brought no answering smile as Marv Crowell walked over to the car. He did manage to say, "Hello, Sue," but he did not sound wild with delight at the sight of her.

Yes, he said, in response to her question, he had heard rumors that she might be coming. "But to tell you the truth, I didn't believe you'd be so foolish."

Instantly she was fighting mad. If what Dave had written her was true, he was a terminally ill man. His letter had touched her heart. At one time, as Marv very well knew, she had hurt his brother badly. Possibly, she conceded, she suffered from a guilt feeling.

"I'll never forget the look in his eyes," she said, "when I told him—"

"Let's not rake up the past," Marv interrupted. "I'm talking about now—and you." Then he pulled open the car door. "Let's go into my place and talk this over." When she hesitated, he took her arm determinedly.

The cottage living room was a pleasant place, the shelves stacked with books and legal papers. Yes, he said, this was where he lived. He liked being by himself, liked quiet when he wanted to read or go over some of his law cases without interruption. He even liked cooking for himself. "And besides, I never felt as if I really belonged up in the family mansion."

There was no hint of self-pity in the words. It was simply a statement of fact, and Sue knew what he meant.

Marv was Martha's son by her first husband. Dave's father, her second husband, had been the one with the wealthy father who had left his fortune in trust for Dave, his grandson. There had been times, Sue guessed, when Marv as a child had been made to feel like an interloper.

Marv told Sue to sit down. He disappeared into the kitchen while she sat wondering about his strange reaction to her arrival. For it *was* strange. It was not so much that he did not seem overjoyed. That was understandable. But there was more to it than that, something sort of mysterious.

She was still trying to figure it out when he returned with coffee, offered her cigarettes, drew up a chair facing hers, and said bluntly: "I wish you hadn't come, Sue."

"Why?"

"It may prove to be a serious mistake. And please let's skip the errand of mercy bit." He did not, he said, mean that unkindly.

It had been a kind, a truly wonderful thing for her to do. Without question, Dave would be happy to see her. And yes, he was a sick man, a very sick man. "Dave and I," he reminded her, "were always very close. I love the guy. It gets me, every time I go in to visit him. He's changed so these last few months he—oh, well, I guess you know what I mean."

His face worked. It was a minute before he could go on. When he did, his voice held a sudden appeal. It was almost as if he were begging her as he caught her hands and said: "Sue, don't go through with it. Let me take you back to your car; then turn around and go back where you came from. Will you do that?"

"Without seeing Dave?" Her tone was shocked. "Do you think I drove across the continent without giving it any thought? Now that I'm here—" She struggled for words to express what was becoming a vast irritation.

"I have my reasons, Sue."

"What reasons?"

"I don't feel free to tell you. I'll say this much—there has been an unexpected development, something that may come as a shock. If you persist in going on with this plan, you'll soon find out for yourself. Believe me, Sue, it would be doing yourself a favor if you'd take my advice. Just forget the whole thing."

She stood up, breathed deeply, and said flatly that she had no intention of taking his advice. "I have no idea what you're talking about, and you refuse to tell me."

As she headed for the door, Marv caught her arms. His fiercely dark eyes were hot on her face. "One reason I won't explain is that it probably wouldn't do any good. You'd go right ahead, even if you knew it meant walking into trouble. You always were too stubborn and headstrong for your own good. I said so the night you insisted we must never see each other again. Didn't I?"

Sue's heart gave a sudden painful lurch. So he did remember!

But she kept her head and her voice under cool control. "You said you didn't want to talk about the past."

"Right. I did say that. So we'll stick to the present, and I'll put it this way. Ever hear of a devil brew?"

When she stared at him silently, he went on: "If you don't know what that means, you'll soon find out."

For a moment they stood in a pool of silence, her eyes fixed on his as if caught by a magnet. Then without warning he caught her in his arms, kissed her hard, and just as abruptly let her go.

"I'd like to say one thing more," he said as she stepped out on the small cottage porch.

She turned, found her eyes once more caught in his and heard him say almost angrily: "I've never stopped loving you."

Chapter 2

Her steps lagged as Sue went slowly up the white stone steps of the beautiful white house. Her eyes were on the entrance door. She stared at it with a worried, anxious expression, reminding herself that it still wasn't too late to turn back. But it would be, once she lifted that gleaming brass knocker. She had been uncertain about this trip from the start. Now, after Marv's vague, mysterious talk, she felt more unsure than ever. What had he been trying to tell her, warn her about?

She lifted the brass knocker.

She had hoped that Martha would see her and come rushing to greet her. Or if not Martha, it would have been nice to see Edith Garber's plump, rosy-cheeked, kindly face. Edith had been the Harding housekeeper for twenty years and more.

The dark-skinned maid wearing a crisp white cap was young and pretty, with an impudent air and way of talking.

"I've got my orders," she said, barring Sue's entrance. "Mrs. Harding is out. Nobody gets in here without her say-so, and she ain't said nothing about a nurse coming."

Sue was puzzled. Was this simply a matter of a new, inexperienced maid throwing her weight around?

"I can assure you Mrs. Harding expects me," she said pleasantly. "Will she be gone long?"

The girl couldn't say. "Some days she stays for quite a spell, like when she goes to the Blue Tavern and—well, meets some of her old pals and all. You know?"

Martha? The Blue Tavern?

Even in the old days, that had been a notorious hangout for the wealthy drinking crowd. Sue could not imagine Martha, with her gentle ways and strict standards of behavior, setting foot in such a place.

She was more and more puzzled.

"Well," she suggested, her manner still friendly, "I assume Mr. Dave Harding is home. He is the one I've come to nurse, and since we're old friends, suppose I go right up to his room. Okay?"

"Nope." Nobody, but nobody, was to see Mr. Harding without Mrs. Harding's say-so. "I got my orders. You'll just have to go away and come back later."

The dark maid appeared about to slam the door in her face. That did it.

Sue had not come three thousand miles to have the door shut against her by an insolent girl who seemed to imagine she owned the house during her employer's absence.

Seething with anger, Sue pushed the door wide

open and pushed her way into the wide, square entrance hall where a gorgeous Oriental rug covered the marble floor.

"I'm going upstairs to Mr. Harding," she said. "If you try to stop me—well, like most nurses, I know a few judo tricks. Do I make myself clear?"

It was amusing to see the look of alarm in the girl's dark eyes.

Sue went up the circular staircase. Halfway up, she could look down into the drawing room to the right of the big hall. It was elegantly furnished with fine old antique pieces and more Oriental rugs. The seventeen-year-old girl she once had been had thought it must be the most beautiful room in the world.

She came to the door at the far end of the upstairs hall. When she opened it, she had her first glimpse of Dave. Wrapped in a bathrobe, he was sitting in a reclining chair staring out of the window, unaware of the door opening. He looked the picture of dejection.

Swiftly crossing the room, Sue murmured, "Hello, Dave," and touched his shoulder lovingly. "You asked me to come, and here I am."

Tears lay behind her smile as she saw the glow in his eyes when he looked up and saw her. He struggled to his feet to put his arms around her.

"Oh, darling, my beautiful darling! You cared enough about me to come." His arms around her trembled, and as he brushed his cheek against hers she felt his hot tears.

She felt racked with pity and compassion. It was as if the storm of a man's pent-up emotions were breaking over her and she did not know how to curb it.

He wanted to hold her a little away and study her face, then tell her how beautiful she was. She was even more beautiful than he remembered her. And when she said lightly, "Now, Dave, I'm no beauty; I never was," he grabbed her back to his heart to groan: "To me you're the most beautiful girl in the world. You always were, you always will be."

He looked emaciated. Sue, watching him, felt drenched with pity as she thought of the bronzed, muscular, god-like young man who had once scraped acquaintance with her on a beach. Now he could have passed for a wasted old man. Even his once handsome young face looked old, the lustre gone from the gray eyes which had once sparkled with the joy of living.

"Now listen," she said, for about the tenth time. "We have so much to talk about, let's go sit down."

"Not yet." He was clutching her hand as if he feared she might vanish once he let go.

"But I have a lot of questions to ask." She wanted to know why Martha wasn't there to greet her. And why she had had practically to force her way into the house.

"The questions will wait, sweetheart."

"Well, how about a cup of coffee?" she persisted, noticing the pot simmering on the electric grill beside his desk. "I'm cold."

"Let my arms warm you." And he pulled her to him again.

What could she do? Shrink away as if she found his embrace repulsive? His eyes were the eyes of a beggar, pleading for a small taste of warmth and affection. It would be cruel to deny him.

"I want you to promise me one thing, Sue."

"If I can, I will.

"Oh, you can. But it may be difficult."

"Don't start talking in riddles, honey." She had had enough of that with Marv and with the maid. "Just tell me what this promise is about."

"Promise you'll stay here with me to the end, *no matter what anyone says or does.*"

It was a curious request which seemed to make no sense. She put it down to the irrational fear of a desperately ill man, and told him without hesitation: "Of course I'll stay, Dave. Did you think I crossed the continent just to call on you for an hour's social visit?"

His arms tightened around her. Again she felt his tears on her cheek as he whispered: "Thank you, my wonderful darling."

Then she heard the voice of a woman who had opened the door noiselessly. "Well, well, look what my hubby's up to." With the voice came amused, sultry laughter. "As the old saying goes, when the cat's away, the mice will play."

Without a word, Dave let go of Sue. He staggered like a drunken man as he made his way to a wide sofa. Sinking down on it, he sat bent over, shaking hands pressed against his eyes. "Oh, God," he muttered.

Sue, completely bewildered, turned to look at the woman attached to the voice. She had pale gold hair hanging loose and eyelids smeared so thickly with blue shadow that her face looked like a mask. With black velvet pants she wore gold slippers and a gold lame blouse.

"But I suppose I must forgive my sweetie." Ignoring Sue as if she were so much empty air, the lush blonde went swiftly to Dave. She had long legs, and she moved like a fashion model. When she sat down, curving one tanned arm around Dave's shoulders, he turned to look at her out of sick, fearful eyes.

Desperately afraid eyes, Sue thought, and heard him saying: "Save the play-acting for your TV commercials, Gloria." He pulled away from her arm as if her touch revolted him. "What do you want now?"

"You know perfectly well what I want, love." Her theatrical voice oozed warmth, but her eyes glancing in Sue's direction were as cold and hard as a pair of stones.

"I want my son—*our* son—to come to us. I want my boy to know his daddy before it's too late. But first, how about introducing your wife to your girl friend?"

Sue, puzzled and amazed by this curious conversation, turned toward the door.

Dave's voice, dull and without hope, called her back. "Don't go, Sue. I might as well get this over with.

"This is my wife, Gloria. We were married seven years ago. After two months, she walked out on me. When she heard I was on my last legs, she walked back in again, with the news that I have a son I never heard of. Now you know."

With that, Dave buried his face in his hands while Gloria gave a husky laugh. "And I know who you are, pet. You're Susan Whittier, the girl my Davey once imagined himself in love with. Just a severe attack of puppy love, of course."

"Shut up," muttered Dave. "What do you know about love?"

"Practically everything, sweetie." The hard, cold eyes drifted back to Susan, who had pulled up a chair simply because she felt too weak with shock to stand.

"If you imagine Dave didn't marry me because he was mad about me, Susan dear—" Gloria interrupted herself to get a cigarette from her bag and fit it into a long jade holder. "As I started to say, you could not possibly be that stupid. As I understand it, you're a nurse. Right?"

"Yes. I'm a nurse."

"Well, there you have it. A nurse learns the facts of life. Therefore you must realize that my Dave forgot all about you long, long ago. As a matter of fact—" more low, sultry laughter—"I'm very sure he forgot your existence the very first time his eyes met mine. If you'll excuse the crude expression, the darling was mine, in the bag, from that very first night."

She blew a stream of smoke rings. "It's a safe bet he never gave you another thought until he discovered he was dying. Then he needed a nurse. So he remembered his long lost love. He wrote you, and you came flying back, and here you are."

Abruptly Gloria rose and came to stand directly in front of Sue before she snapped, in a curt, completely changed tone: "It might interest you to know that I'm now in charge of this house. I'm the boss. Understand?"

Sue looked at her levelly. "If you are saying you don't want me here, fine." She stood up, glancing at Dave, who still sat bent over, saying not a word. "But before I go, I must insist on seeing Martha."

"You can't see her."

"Why not?"

"Because she's ill and isn't allowed to see anyone."

"*Who* won't allow her to see anyone?"

"I won't." The words came like the crack of a whip. "Didn't I just say I was the boss?" She added casually, as if it were a matter of little importance, that Martha had days when she didn't seem right in the head. "I may have to send her to a rest home."

"Like fun you'll send my mother away," snapped Dave, coming suddenly to life. He struggled to his feet, his face working savagely. "And you won't send Sue away, either. If you try it, you'll wish you hadn't. I may be dying, but I'm not dead yet. Remember that."

Suddenly, turning to him, Gloria was all smiles and purring sweetness. She could change her approach, thought Sue, as an actress changed costumes.

"Now darling, I never said that Sue couldn't stay. I was merely suggesting that if she wanted to stay, if *you* have your heart set on her staying, perhaps we could make a little deal. How about that, sweetie?"

"What kind of a deal?" His voice was surprisingly strong, but Sue, watching him, saw clammy sweat break out over his face. She thought that any minute he might collapse, and sheer hatred coiled like a snake inside her; hate for what this woman with her shining pale gold hair and her cold, ruthless eyes was doing to him.

"Can't you guess, dear Davey?" Gloria spread her soft, beautifully cared for hands.

What she wanted was to have her son—"our son"—come and live with them and get to know and love his daddy before it was too late. "So he can remember his own father, once you're gone."

Sue was fairly certain she was going to scream if this awful woman mentioned Dave's approaching death one more time.

Gloria fitted a fresh cigarette into the long holder. Then she said it was utter nonsense for Dave to object that he was too weak and ill to deal with a noisy six-year-old problem boy. "It isn't as if he were retarded or anything like that, sweetie. Actually, Bobby is unusually bright for his age. His only problem is that he's inclined to be a psychopathic liar, and that needn't bother you." She tapped off cigarette ash and wheeled around to ask Sue:

"Since you're a nurse, I suppose you know that lots of kids do a lot of lying. Right?"

Sue nodded distractedly, her worried eyes still on Dave, who croaked: "What's the deal you have in mind?"

"Let me bring Bobby to stay with us, and I'll permit your old girl firend to stay and act as nurse.

"On a temporary basis," she added. Then started screaming at the top of her lungs. "He's dying! Do something, for God's sake do something. Maybe he's had a heart attack and he's dead."

In his effort to struggle back to the sofa, Dave had swayed dizzily, clutched at the air, and collapsed. He was stretched out on the floor, unconscious. Leaning down, Sue felt his pulse. It was irregular, but not dangerously so. Hypoglycemin, she suspected; lack of protein in the blood which often complicated malignancy in the white blood cells. A patient could collapse, go into a coma, without a moment's warning. But it wasn't fatal.

"Shut up," she snapped at the blonde woman who was still wailing like a banshee. "Get some milk and cheese. When he comes to, he'll need something on his stomach."

"He's dying!"

"He may die, at that," Sue said flatly, "if we don't give him some milk as soon as possible." Frowning, she looked up and was amazed to see Gloria's look of sick terror. Her skin had gone a pasty white; under smeared lipstick her lips were gray. She looked ready to pass out, she was so frightened.

Why? Sue wondered.

Chapter 3

Because she was past being surprised at anything, Sue was not greatly surprised when Martha appeared—a small, briskly moving little woman with fluffy white hair. She was carrying a tray with a bottle of milk and a glass. Not taking time even to say hello, she handed the tray to Sue.

"I just woke up from a long nap," she said, "and heard you ask for milk."

Then she knelt by Dave, her face drawn with sorrow and worry over this son who was dearer to her than life.

"It isn't that I ever loved Dave more than Marv," she explained to Sue. "It was—oh, call it a different kind of love. Marv had always been so strong and self-reliant, able to look after himself. Dave was the weak one; charming, handsome, sensitive and sweet, but weak.

"Dave needed me more."

This conversation took place late that afternoon. Dave had regained consciousness. Then the doctor had come, a Dr. Ronald Brown.

Sue hadn't been favorably impressed by Dr. Brown. He was youngish, with a silky little black mustache. She was even less impressed when she learned that Martha's old family doctor had been dismissed. Gloria had decided Dave should have a younger doctor, one with more modern, up-to-date ideas.

Dr. Brown seemed to have quite a few modern ideas, but how sound they were, or how much he actually knew about treating a man in Dave's condition—Sue had her doubts.

When she mentioned hypoglycemin, for instance, the man gave no sign that he understood what she was talking about.

He did, however, give Dave a shot of something or other. He left some medication. He patted Gloria's arm, commending her on her bravery, her patience. Then, with a flashing white smile, he was gone.

After Dave fell into a deep natural sleep, Martha took Sue in hand, leading the way to a room directly across the hall. Announcing that she felt terribly ill, and armed with sleeping pills, provided by Dr. Brown, and the air of a tragedy queen, Gloria had gone to her own room.

"And now," Martha was saying, "when he needs me more than ever, that awful woman is threatening to put me out of the house." Her voice shook, and helpless tears came.

Sue sat on the wide maple bed with the rose-colored spread which she remembered so well. Martha sat in the small antique slipper chair, just as she used to do in the old days when Sue stayed there overnight and Martha would come in for a confidential chat before they went to bed.

In some ways they had been as close as mother and daughter. To be here now, in the deepening twilight, with Martha pouring her heart out should have been like coming home. Only she had come home to sickness, sorrow, and some all-pervading evil which she still could not understand.

"You can't be serious," Sue said, laughing to cover her shock and concern. "This is your home. How could anybody put you out of it?"

"It's not mine, Sue. Legally, this property belongs to Dave." According to his grandfather's will, Martha explained, the house was left to Dave, and also most of the old man's fortune. The money was left in trust, of course, until Dave was thirty years old.

Martha gave a long, deep sigh. "He was thirty his last birthday," she said, and got up to close the drapes and switch on lights which bathed the room in a soft glow.

Then, somewhat to Sue's smiling surprise, she went to a closet and produced a bottle of brandy. "You know something, honey?" For a moment she seemed her old self: Pert, spirited, full of spice and vinegar.

"In my young years I was never a juvenile delinquent. But it's never too late to start, even at my ripe old age. So how about us having a little snort?"

Bringing glasses and water from the bathroom, she perched on the bed beside Sue. "And I think I'd like to try one of your cigarettes."

Smiling, Sue got a fresh pack from her bag. Since Martha seemed suddenly in a more cheerful mood, maybe she shouldn't bother her with troublesome questions. But she must. She simply must know the facts about Dave and Gloria, and what she would be up against if she stayed.

She asked: "Is that woman really Dave's wife?"

Martha nodded; her face seemed to crumple. "Oh, yes," she said, gagging over a swallow of brandy. "She's his wife, Sue. They were married about three months after you left."

"But why didn't you write me about it, Martha?"

The woman gave a deep sigh. "Because I knew from the start it was an awful mistake. I was afraid you'd feel you were responsible. So I decided it was best to keep it to myself."

She got up to turn off one lamp, turn off another. Then she went for more water, opened the hall door to see if there was any sound from Dave's room. "I'm nervous as a witch," she said, coming back to the bed.

"I suppose I'd better tell you the whole story," she said, clutching Sue's hand, "right from the start."

In some ways it was a very old story, the story of a highly emotional man who seemed to crack up when he lost the girl he loved.

"He walked out of this house one night," Martha said. He just packed his bags and left, without a word to her about leaving, about where he was going.

For a solid three months she didn't know where he was. He didn't write, didn't phone. Needless to say, she was half out of her mind with sorrow.

She had considered hiring a detective to find out something about him. Marv had advised against that.

"Marv argued that Dave was an adult. He was old enough to make his own decisions. If he wanted to disappear for a while, live his own life free of restraint, even if he chose to get into trouble, I had no right to try to stop him or pry into what he was doing."

Later, she added, she discovered that Marv had known right along where Dave was.

He had known that Dave had taken an expensive Hollywood apartment, that he had gotten in with a crowd who spent their time drinking, smoking marijuana, driving to Vegas to gamble over weekends, swimming in the nude. Martha's hand was shaky as she raised her glass to her lips, found it empty, and poured a little more brandy.

Marv, she learned later, had gone to see Dave, tried to talk a little sense into his head. But the sad fact was that Dave never seemed sober enough to grasp what Marv was saying.

And all that time, Martha said, she had been in the dark, just wondering and worrying and waiting—until the day when Dave came home and brought with him this blonde person with her grotesque make-up and her slinky way of walking, wearing the wedding ring Dave had put on her finger.

"I could see she was vulgar and cheap," Martha said. One glance had told her that. But Dave had married her during a week-end at Vegas, and she had decided to make the best of it.

Sue interrupted to ask: "You mean he brought her back here to live with you, at Hillcrest?"

Yes, that was the plan. Obviously Dave had come to his senses. Probably it was the shock of realizing what his riotous living had done. Anyway, he seemed to accept the fact that he had made his bed and it was up to him to lie in it.

Fortunately, Gloria had had no taste for continuing the marriage, if it meant living at Hillcrest and going out of her mind with boredom.

"I suspected at the time," Martha said, "that she walked out on him when she discovered he wouldn't come into any big money until he was thirty."

At that time Dave was only twenty-three. Gloria had been working as a fashion model. She held extravagant ideas about what she considered her ravishing beauty, and she had equally extravagant ideas about becoming a famous TV actress. At any rate, she left him at the end of two or three months.

"And he has never seen her since—until she reappeared two weeks ago and announced that she had had herself appointed Dave's guardian."

"*What?*"

Nodding bleakly, Martha covered her face with

her hands and let the tears come. "Oh, Sue, what am I to do?"

Putting a comforting arm around the thin, shaking shoulders, Sue asked: "But what's this story about Dave having a son?"

"I don't know," Martha sobbed. "She claims she didn't know she was pregnant until after she left Dave. When the boy was born, she didn't let us know because she was afraid we'd take her son away from her. Now she wants to bring him here. And you know as well as I do, Dave is in no condition to have a noisy, probably incorrigible child foisted on him."

"Do you believe her story?" Sue asked, struck by a sudden suspicion.

"Oh, I suppose it's true enough," Martha said, adding that she had no reason to believe Gloria had been promiscuous with men.

The point was, she had used this boy to help get legal control over everything Dave owned. She had gotten some lawyer who went before a judge, claiming that Dave was too incompetent mentally and physically to make any business decisions. To protect the interests of their son, she had asked for power of guardianship and gotten it.

"Now," Martha sobbed, "she's scheming to get me out of my home, threatens to send me off to a rest home."

"But she can't, Martha. This is your home, and I simply don't believe—" Sue interrupted herself to ask: "What does Marv say about all this? He's a lawyer. Surely he doesn't believe she can get away with anything so outrageous."

"I can't get Marv to say much one way or the other. He just keeps telling me to play it cool. He says she is a very shrewd, clever woman, and I'd better play along with her, or pretend to."

Strange, thought Sue. She sat lost in thought after Martha left the room, saying she wanted to freshen up a little before dinner.

She would have taken Marv Crowell for more of a fighter.

Chapter 4

There was nothing about the charming white cottage, with the rose garden in front, to suggest that it was occupied by Mrs. Ethel Kent, a British medium who was famous for her clairvoyant powers and ability to give astonishing predictions concerning the future. Nor did the slight gray-haired woman in blue jeans on her knees weeding between the bushes resemble in any way the traditional image of a phony fortune teller, perhaps because she was not a phony.

When Gloria parked her car in front of the house around four that afternoon, she wondered if she had come to the wrong address. She had gotten the address from a friend in Hollywood, a fairly successful actress who claimed she never made a move without consulting Ethel Kent, who was an absolute marvel. "She's uncanny, darling, absolutely uncanny."

The white-haired woman stood up. Noticing Gloria staring at her from her car, she walked to the gate of the white picket fence. Her smile was lovely; her remarkable eyes seemed to illumine her plain face.

"Were you looking for someone?" she asked pleasantly.

"Yes," Gloria said. "For a Mrs. Ethel Kent. But I must have the wrong address. You aren't a fortune teller, are you?"

The smile seemed to reach those glowing eyes. "No, dear. I don't tell fortunes, not in the usual sense. But at times I am able to see things that most folks do not see. I am able occasionally to offer advice about the future. Would you like to come in?"

"Sure," Gloria said, adding that she could use some honest to goodness advice. "I'm about to go off my trolley, figuring what to do about a couple of little matters."

"You should try to relax," said Mrs. Kent, leading the way into a white-carpeted room which seemed like a haven of peace and rest.

This pervading atmosphere was completely lost on Gloria, who was not in search of either peace or rest. What she wanted to know was how not to make any false moves and so let a fortune slip out of her hands.

"Close your eyes and take several deep breaths, dear. That will help you relax and get in tune with the infinite," said Mrs. Kent, and went off to wash her hands while Gloria sat down, lit a fresh cigarette, and wondered if she was wasting her time with a real kook.

When the woman returned, she directed Gloria into a kind of alcove furnished with a desk, two chairs, and a tall vase filled with roses on a small filing cabinet.

They sat facing each other.

More and more convinced that this whole deal was for the birds, Gloria watched the clairvoyant relax, kick off her shoes and take a few of the deep breaths she had recommended, while she closed her eyes and let her shoulders slump.

Gloria wondered if she was going into a trance. She certainly wanted none of *that* nonsense. What she should do was get out of that joint, but fast. As she gazed in disgust at the apparently sleeping woman, she was thinking about Marv Crowell and wondering if he would be home in the cottage by six o'clock.

Marv was, she felt pretty sure, her best bet. He was attracted to her, had given every sign that he could go for her in a big way. So it stood to reason she could get around him, persuade him to play along with the little deal she had in mind. If she played her cards right, persuading him should be an easy matter, since he would have plenty to gain and nothing to lose.

She reminded herself—and she would definitely remind him—that it didn't seem fair that Dave should inherit all the Harding money while he, Marv, was left out in the cold. What if Marv was only a half-brother and not related to Grandfather Harding, who had made and left the money? He was part of the family, he was Dave's brother. So it seemed only fair that he should get a cut. That was the way Gloria looked at it.

Mrs. Kent's eyes opened.

"Why do I see money lying all around you?" she asked. "Such a lot of money. Some of it tied up in bundles, some all loose as if thousand-dollar bills were flying all over the place. My, I never did see so much money." The eyes closed again. "I seem to see you down on your hands and knees, trying to grab some of the bills."

"Do I get them?"

The eyes opened again. "Dear, this is very strange. I see a little round ball, like a tiny little moon. It seems to glow, and it darts around as if it were alive, first in one direction, then another. I can't see where the little ball comes from or how it got there, but there it is. It practically dances. And it comes between you and all the packets of money. You reach for a bundle, and the little ball darts around and stops you from getting it. Isn't that curious?"

Curious, my eye, thought Gloria. So much gobbledygook, that was what the old gal's phony line added up to. Still, she had seen the money.... That part was sort of peculiar.

"Do I get the money?" That was the main point at issue.

Mrs. Kent looked at her for a moment, her eyes thoughtful. "My dear," she said presently, "I think you want me to tell you that you will come into a large fortune, that everything will work out beautifully." She smiled a bit sadly.

That, she said, was what many of her clients wanted to hear. Laden with their secret hopes and desires, and all too often their greed, they came to her to be told that their every wish would be granted. Unfortunately, she was not a fairy godmother. Nor was she a charlatan who aimed primarily to send a customer away feeling happy and pleased.

"Things come to me in pictures," she said. "I can only tell you what I see. I do not see you getting the money. Unhappily, I seem to see confusion and trouble all around you."

She closed her eyes again. "Dear me, there goes that little ball again. Such a beautiful, glittering little ball. But it keeps standing in the way of everything you want. I wish I could think what it means."

Her eyes opened again. "Have you any idea what it means, dear?"

Disgusted, Gloria stood up. "I think," she said rather sneeringly, "it means you're making up a lot of nonsense that doesn't mean a thing."

Walking with her to the door, Mrs. Kent said in a truly troubled voice, "I know how you feel. So many folks react the same way when I cannot tell them what they want to hear. Sometimes, later on, they come back and say they wished they had taken my advice."

"I haven't asked for your advice," Gloria said curtly. "And you haven't given me any; just some nonsense about a ball which you admit you don't understand."

"Perhaps I do know and did not want to tell you." The gentle voice sharpened a trifle. "I think I had better tell you. I have the feeling you are tempted to scramble after something you have no right to. Light is a symbol of good; it is a mystical symbol. Possibly the little ball, glowing with light, doesn't intend for you to get what you want, because it isn't right for you to have it."

Driving off in her car, Gloria was absolutely furious. She must be slipping, throwing away her time and money on that phony. What did that fake know about anything? And why did she have a sudden most unpleasant feeling, as if she were on a steep slope, with her foothold beginning to slip from under her?

Tomorrow she would get the boy here. That was the next step, and she didn't need any advice about it from an old gal who was doubtless half cracked.

Before tomorrow, of course, would come tonight. Tonight she would make it her business to see Marv. Thinking about him, her eyes grew dreamy. She had never fancied herself in love, never once in her whole thirty odd years. Only three things had ever been important to her: making the most of her beauty; using that beauty to attain success as an actress, a goal which still eluded her; and reaching out her hot little hands for money wherever she happened to catch sight of it.

Wouldn't it be something if now at long last she had come on a man who could be really important to her? If she could tie up the man, Marv, and a fortune both in the same little bundle, that would be absolutely wonderful.

Love and money! She sighed happily and kept smiling to herself. What more could a woman ask for?

Chapter 5

After she had unpacked her clothes and taken a quick shower, Sue started to put on a white uniform. Then she changed her mind after Myrtle, the little maid, came to her door, wanting to know when and how dinner should be served. Sara, the cook, she reported, wasn't eager to hang about all evening, waiting for Mrs. Harding to get home and give some instructions. "You want I should bring the stuff up on trays?"

"Mrs. Harding has gone out?" Sue asked, surprised. The last she had seen of Dave's glamorous wife, she had appeared to be dying on her feet.

"Yes, ma'am. She's out. No telling when she'll be back, and like I said—"

Sue interrupted to say that trays would be fine, and then it occurred to her to ask the girl if this was her regular work.

"You mean working in rich people's houses?" The dark head lifted proudly, and for the first time it struck Sue that Myrtle was close to being a beauty, with her coffee-colored skin, large and dark and shining eyes.

It was her impudent, self-assertive manner that

Sue had found so offensive, and she began to understand the reason for that when the girl said a bit contemptuously: "I don't really know a thing about being a maid." Nor did she want to know. "I do TV commercials," she went on, explaining that was how she had become acquainted with Mrs. Harding. "Just between you and me, she isn't much of an actress. But she sure is a good-looker."

Anyway, in one of her own commercials, Myrtle took the part of a maid serving coffee. Mrs. Harding thought she was very cute in the part, so she invited her to come along and act as a maid in her sick husband's "mansion."

"It was such a good deal, I figured I might as well take her up on it," Myrtle said, especially after Mrs. Harding promised her the husband was "practically the same as dead already."

So, mused Sue, returning to the closet to decide what to put on. Faithful old Edith Garber had been fired so that Gloria could bring in an incompetent girl who did not pretend to know anything about housework. Why?

Because Edith had been Martha's dear friend as well as her housekeeper and would never have stood by, silent, while efforts were afoot to force Martha out of her home?

That was Martha's explanation when Sue went to her room after she was dressed. "It's as plain as the nose on your face," said Martha, after telling Sue how pretty she looked in her blue sheath.

"Dave always said blue was your color, Sue.

And as for the way *she* got rid of dear Edith, fired that fine, good woman almost the minute she got her nose inside the door—" Martha's voice sharpened.

Gloria was nothing more or less than a shrewd, malicious schemer. "She's bent and determined to get me out of this house." And the simplest way would be to prove that Dave's poor old mother was losing her mind. She had Ronald Brown, that young squirt of a doctor, right under her thumb. No doubt he would sign commitment papers if Gloria paid him enough to do it. "And with nobody left in this house to testify that I'm anything but feeble-minded—"

Sue drew a chair up beside the bed where Martha had been napping. "She couldn't get away with anything so rotten," Sue said firmly. But her eyes were anxious.

"Couldn't she?" Her small, pixie-like face drawn into about a thousand wrinkles, Martha snapped an abrupt question. "Sue, honey, how much do you know about pills?"

"Pills?"

"That's what I said, dear: pills." She had just been reading a very clever mystery, Martha said, pointing to the paperback on the bed beside her. "It has given me an idea."

In the story, she explained, there was an elderly woman who was as smart, as mentally alert, as the next one. But there was a murderer who wanted to get rid of her. So the old lady was given aspirin pills. Only every second day, there was a wee bit of codein in the pills. The result was that one day the victim would seem to be perfectly normal, and the next her mind would be so blurred that she didn't know what she was saying or doing and couldn't even walk straight. And the upshot of it was—

Smiling, Sue interrupted, reaching for Martha's hand. "Now look, darling. Let's not lose our perspective. It's obvious that Gloria is after Dave's money and will try a lot of schemes to get it. But that doesn't mean she would try to kill you." That, Sue said flatly, she couldn't buy.

"All right." Martha quite agreed, and she hadn't said she believed Gloria intended actually to do her in; only to prove she was a bit batty so as to get her committed to a hospital or institution where she probably would lose her mind in short order.

Tranquilizers, to be exact. "That squirt of a doctor said I needed to calm down," said Martha. Meanwhile, there remained the problem of the pills. "Then he wrote out a prescription for tranquilizers and handed it to Gloria with instructions to make sure I swallowed two of the pills every night before I went to sleep."

Oh, she wasn't denying they helped her sleep. What made her very suspicious was that some mornings she woke up feeling so dizzy, so strange, not like herself at all. Two or three times she had just toppled over while trying to get to the bathroom. When she tried to talk, she couldn't seem to make the words come out right. She would have to get back in bed and stay there the rest of the day.

"What do you think, Sue honey?" Was it possible she was being given some kind of dope to make her act crazy?

Hesitant to make any snap judgment, Sue promised to think about it. Meanwhile, she suggested that Martha hold the prescription pills under her tongue until Gloria left the room. "I'll bring you a glass of warm milk every night with one or two calcium tablets." Many people found that combination relaxing.

Martha is permitting her imagination to get the best of her, Sue thought as she headed for Dave's room. And yet, deep down, she knew that she, too, was suspicious.

Who wouldn't be suspicious of a woman who walked out on her husband after two or three months of marriage, then, after seven years, walked back in again when she learned the husband was at death's door? A moron could figure how all that added up. Before it was too late, she wanted to establish her rights to part of his money.

But the question was, Sue reflected, what rights Gloria had, since she was the one who had abandoned the marriage as casually as a shoe that didn't fit. And if she had some devious scheme in mind, what could it possibly be? And why should she be so set and determined to get Dave's mother out of the house?

It was a question without an answer.

Reminding herself that she was a nurse, that she had better confine herself to looking after Dave and forget the strange goings-on in the house, she took charge of the tray-cart which Myrtle was rolling along the hall.

In his room, Dave was sitting up in bed. His color was better. He assured her that he was feeling fine, just fine. Yes, he felt up to eating those grilled chops, which looked delicious. Anything would look delicious, he added, even a bowl of mush, with Sue sitting beside him.

Unhappily, after a few bites, his appetite vanished. How could he be expected to bother with food when *she* was there, just the way he had dreamed of her? Over and over and over, he had closed his eyes and pictured her sitting there. "I've longed so for you. I've never stopped loving you, darling."

Suddenly his show of emotion was like a storm breaking. Tears flooded his eyes. Sue had to take away the tray. And when she sat on the bed beside him, his trembling hands caught hers in a grip like that of a drowning man clutching a raft. "Let me talk," he pleaded. "Don't tell me it's bad for me to get excited."

Please let him tell her about all that had been locked up in his heart through the long, lonely years. Every man, he told her, must have a dream to hold to. Some dreamed of becoming famous in the world of art or music; some of making a fortune, or of great adventures in far away places, or of finding long lost treasure at the ocean's bottom.

"I've had my dream, too, sweetheart: that some day you would come back to me."

A psychiatrist, Sue mused, would say that he was sick, that his love for his first sweetheart was not love at all, but the obsession of a mixed up, immature man who had never adjusted to reality. The psychiatrist would say that he needed depth analysis, perhaps years of analysis, to find out what this irrational devotion to one girl stemmed from.

Her eyes met Dave's, she felt his trembling hand close over hers, and all she knew for sure was that his love for her was the most real experience in his life. "I wouldn't have missed loving you," he was saying softly. "Even with all the pain and heartbreak, it's been worth it."

He said: "Wherever I go when I leave this world, my love for you will endure for always."

She held back her own tears while she got him fixed for the night. She took his temperature, which was a little above normal, but not much. On the bedside table was a tiny plastic box containing two capsules. Dave said he was supposed to take them the last thing before going to sleep.

"Sit here beside me," he begged, and he lay for a time just gazing at her. Once he said: "I wanted to explain to you about Gloria," but Sue stopped him with a firm shake of her head.

"Martha told me all about your marriage," she said. And as for asking her advice about bringing the boy there, the son he had never seen—again a firm shake of her head. "I haven't any right to advise you about that, Dave, although—" She hesitated, uncertain how to frame the question.

"Haven't you any desire to see this boy?" she asked finally. "After all, since he is your own son—"

"Yes, I know." It was normal, wasn't it, for a man to want to see the child who was really part of himself? But, he said, his tone thoughtful, a trifle puzzled, possibly he wasn't normal. "I just can't get the feeling that I actually have a son. You know?"

They discussed this for a few minutes. Then, his eyes filled with a heartbreaking longing, Dave whispered: "Won't you kiss me good night, darling, for old times' sake?"

She bent forward, her smile warm and tender with compassion as she smoothed his hair back from his hot forehead. She put her arms around him, holding him close, as a mother might hold a hurt child who was very precious to her.

He was very precious to her, as if he were a beloved brother, or the dearest friend she had ever known. With all her heart she wished that she could have given him the intense, passionate form of love which he had wanted from her.

"Good night, Dave," she whispered, her lips gentle against his.

He fell asleep in her arms.

As she left him, her eyes were blurred with hot tears. She was remembering a song from an old movie: "A Song of Love is a Sad Song."

It could be the saddest song in the world.

Chapter 6

In her own room Sue walked the floor, worrying, wondering for about the thousandth time if coming back to Hillcrest had been a big mistake. Of what real use was she? Dave was slowly dying. Transfusions, new drugs had kept him going—if you could call it that. They might even keep him breathing for several more months, with luck—again if you could call it luck. But a leukemia patient could never get well, and there was next to nothing a nurse could do for him.

The fact was, Dave did not need a nurse. What he needed was rest for his body, peace for his troubled mind; not tears in his eyes, not an emotional storm every time he gazed into the flashing blue eyes of the girl who had been his sweetheart long, long ago.

My being here, Sue mused, may be the worst possible thing for him.

She walked to the window. It had started to drizzle, which made it a fine night for a walk. She had always loved to walk in the rain.

From behind the line of evergreens at the far side of the house, she could see the light from the guest cottage.

The trees brought back memories.

They had been planted on the very first day Dave brought her to Hillcrest. Martha had invited her to luncheon, because she couldn't wait to meet the girl Dave had been "raving about."

The food had been delicious; the table, set with glittering silver and fine, fragile china, had looked like a picture. Sue had never seen a table so grand. She could scarcely eat, she was so impressed, and so afraid of using the wrong fork or spoon.

Dave, directly across the table, couldn't eat either. He was too engaged in watching her, his heart in his eyes.

When luncheon was over, Dave had walked her outside to see the grounds. That was when she first met Marv, the brother who had not joined them in the dining room, he explained, because he was too busy helping the gardener get the trees planted.

"Hi, Sue," he said, and she was aware of a muscular man, stripped to the waist, sweat glistening over his shoulders and chest. She was also aware of fiercely dark eyes which seemed to take in all he needed to see of her in one probing glance.

He did smile, just once, with a flash of white teeth. "If I happened to be a ladies man, I might try to take you away from Dave." But the fact was, he hadn't any time for girls. He was too busy with his law books and various odd jobs he took on, not to mention helping keep these grounds in shape.

Then he went back to digging a hole for one of

the evergreens, and Sue wondered why, with all the Harding money, one brother was out there working like a handy man, sweating like a horse.

It was not until later that she learned that Marv was a half-brother whose own father had left only a pittance of insurance money. His pride being as fierce as his dark eyes, he wanted no part of the money his mother had gotten through a second marriage. At the age of eleven, or possibly twelve, Marv had decided he must earn what he wanted in this life, even money for his education.

This was very noble of him. Sue supposed it showed a fine character. But by the time she heard the whole story she had decided that Marv Crowell was rude and seemed to go out of his way to ignore her existence. And at the little party Martha gave to announce her and Dave's engagement, Marv didn't even have the politeness to put in an appearance.

All in all, the man was impossible.

She decided that she thoroughly disliked him—and then came the night when they went walking on the beach.

Leaving the window, Sue got her blue plastic raincoat from the closet. She went down the stairs and out of the house, delighting in the cool, gentle feel of the rain against her face. Nothing was farther from her mind than a visit with Marv. But as luck would have it, just as she reached the gravel path leading up to the cottage the gentle little rain became a furious downpour, and the wind that came with it practically blew her up the path to the cottage door.

Marv opened the door. He said, of course Sue must come in until the storm was over.

Sue did not get the impression that her arrival filled him with unqualified delight, and yet—perhaps her imagination was working overtime.

Unquestionably he was friendly, and concerned for fear she'd take cold from getting drenched to the skin. He took her into his living room, which was small and cozy, with shabby easy chairs and a wood fire burning cheerfully behind brass andirons.

After a glance at her raincoat, ripped and torn by the raging wind, he said that might as well go in the trash. And her dress had better come off, too, and her slippers, which were soaked. He disappeared, then reappeared with a dark woolen bathrobe. "Put that on," he directed, while he went to fix a drink to warm her up.

Marv's phone was in a tiny alcove between the sitting room and kitchen. It rang just as she sat down to take off her sodden slippers.

She couldn't help hearing what he was saying, and the word "no" summed up almost everything that he had to say.

His girl friend, Sue concluded, feeling somehow depressed at the thought. Never, she decided, had she heard a more perfect example of a man trying to make a girl understand it was impossible for him to meet her, or go somewhere with her, or whatever, without saying much of anything.

Once he did go so far as to murmur: "I'm really sorry, dear. But—"

"I'm terribly sorry," she said when he came back carrying a tray with glasses, brandy, and a siphon bottle of soda.

"Sorry about what?" He put the tray on an antique table, once a cobbler's bench, in front of the fire.

"Why pretend?" Sue asked with a smile. "I'm interfering with a date. Right?"

"Wrong." He drew up a chair facing hers.

She had never considered Marv a handsome man, certainly not in the pretty-boy sense of the word. But there was something strangely fascinating about him. Years ago, she mused ruefully, it had been an attraction strong enough to change her whole life. And the pull, the charm, whatever it was, had never died. She knew that as their eyes met, and her crazy, unruly heart began to skip and jerk.

"If you can call her back," Sue suggested, "I can get out of here, fast." It wouldn't kill her to run back to the house, she said. Since she was already soaking wet, a little more water wouldn't matter.

He scowled, as if bored with her foolish remarks. How much soda did she want with the brandy? That question having been settled, he noticed that her stockings were still on. This sent him to his knees to strip them off her. Since she was supposed to be a nurse, she should have sense enough to know that wet feet could be a terrible health hazard.

"Now put your feet up on that brass railing," he ordered. He fussed over her a few minutes longer, getting a towel to dry her dark hair, rubbing until it sprang into natural waves. Then she had to have some more brandy; maybe this time some hot coffee laced with brandy.

At first his concern seemed very sweet. Sue was not accustomed to being treated like a delicate flower that might perish if blown by a rough wind. It was a nice change.

But the change became a bit boring after fifteen minutes or so. More than that, she was suddenly suspicious.

Marv seemed to be jumping up and down, doing every conceivable thing he could think of to avoid settling down to a serious talk.

Why?

Was he afraid of questions she might ask about Dave and the return of his long-lost wife? If that was it, why should he be afraid? Of what?

When he returned with the coffee, Sue blurted in sudden irritation: "Listen, my friend, you're making me nervous. I'm not going to melt because I got wet. But I am likely to go out of my mind if you don't sit down, stay put, and answer a few questions."

"Such as?"

"I need to know a little about what's truly going on, Marv."

She leaned toward him. Perhaps, she went on, it had been a mistake for her to come back. Possibly she should have taken his advice this morning and left without trying to see Dave. She hadn't known then, still didn't know, what was the wise, sensible course.

But she was there, and she seemed to have walked into a house of mystery. She found Martha worried sick about being put out of her home.

Marv interrupted instantly: "Mother can always come here with me."

"But it would break her heart to leave Dave. You know that, Marv."

And what about Gloria? She didn't seem the type who would be interested in anything but getting her share of Dave's estate. "Yet when he fainted suddenly that afternoon, I never saw a woman look so terrified. If it's his money she's after, you'd think the sooner he went, the better pleased she'd be."

Marv's smile was slow, inscrutable. "Yes," he said, "one would think that. So possibly you're wrong about her." Gloria's story, when she returned, had been that she had loved Dave when she married him, that she had never stopped loving him, that she would have returned to make up long ago except that her pride had kept her from coming. She had lived with the hope that some day, sooner or later, he would come after her. But when she discovered that time was running out—

"Marv Crowell!" Sue's tone was scornful. "Do you expect me to believe that you swallow that phony story?"

"Ah, well—" again the enigmatic smile—"I have heard tell that gals in general are quick to believe the worst of a glamorous blonde. Possibly that's your trouble."

He got up to get more coffee, while Sue sat glowering angrily at nothing.

Chapter 7

Marv Crowell specialized in criminal law. Already, at the age of thirty-four, he had made something of a name for himself as an excellent defense attorney. That same afternoon, Sue had listened to Martha boast a bit about his success. "I guess," she had said, smiling proudly, "Marv is the kind who can talk a jury into believing that black is white."

Fine.

But I don't happen to be sitting on a jury, Sue mused. So why should he try to convince *her* that Dave's gorgeous wife, with her pale shining hair and her cold hard eyes, was simply the victim of an unhappy childhood experience?

"Pitiful," said Sue. Her tone implied that she didn't believe a word he was saying. It implied further that she did not believe that *he* believed it.

This was after Marv had brought in the coffee which Sue declined. He had settled himself with his pipe, his legs stretched out to the fire, and smiled that enigmatic smile which for some reason infuriated Sue. He said: "From what she tells me, Gloria went through an ordeal when she was no more than four which scarred her to the depths of her soul."

"Touching."

"Want to hear her story?"

"Not especially."

"You'd better let me tell you." It might, Marv said, give her a better understanding of what made Gloria tick.

Still with that cryptic smile, he recrossed his legs, refilled his pipe, resettled himself in the easy chair. Never had she seen a man look more comfortable, as if he were thoroughly enjoying himself.

One thing it would help her to understand, Marv said, was why Gloria had never allowed Dave to know he had a son. When little more than a baby, Gloria had been used as a weapon between two parents who hated each other. During the divorce proceedings, poor little Gloria had been dragged from court to court. Photographs of the beautiful, sad little child had appeared on a thousand front pages. When it was all over, the father, a wealthy man, had won custody of the little girl.

All of this, naturally, had given Gloria plenty of hard, embittering knowledge as to the power of money when a child's future was at stake. "She said to me, and I quote, 'A mother's love simply doesn't count.'

"So there," said Marv, "you have a simple and logical explanation as to why Dave was never told about this boy. Gloria, so she claims, was absolutely terrified that Dave would use his money to get the kid away from her."

"I see." But what she did not see, said Sue, was why Gloria couldn't have used her own money to fight back, if necessary. "It works both ways. Right?"

Marv shifted his legs again, seeming to have a bit of a problem with his pipe. "But she didn't have any money, Sue, except what she was making as a model, and from occasional TV commercials. All of which added up to a fairly precarious living, especially since she was not getting any younger."

Generally speaking, he pointed out, a model was done for by the time she was thirty.

"What about the wealthy father?"

There, Marv conceded, her account was a bit vague. Explaining that it made her very bitter and unhappy to go into detail, Gloria had simply told him that once he got custody, her dad hadn't wanted to be bothered with her. He had spent his money on liquor, other women, and the race tracks. Presently he died broke. Her dear sweet mummy had also died, presumably of a broken heart, complicated by peneumonia, a kidney infection, and varicose veins. The result of it was that by the time she was fifteen, Gloria was all alone in the world.

"Sad."

"Yes, wasn't it?" Marv smiled, watching Sue's expression of scornful disbelief. "Don't you believe what I've told you, Sue?"

"Do you believe it?"

For once Marv's mouth lost the smile and he spoke with apparent sincerity. In his work, he said, he had learned not to be too quick to pass judgment. A defense attorney had to recognize that there were two sides to every story, and that people were not always what they seemed to be.

The phone rang again. Marv chose to ignore it. And when Sue reached for her slippers and nylons, he took the slippers away from her.

"We'd better finish this discussion," he said.

Sue said flatly there was nothing more to discuss.

She had come back to Hillcrest to serve as Dave's nurse. It was her job to do that to the best of her ability. It was not up to her to pass judgment on the lady in question. For all she knew, the gal was a pathetic, misunderstood creature with a heart overflowing with mother love and wings about to sprout any minute.

"But I do not have to like her, or believe this sob story." She grabbed her slippers, put them on, and stood up. "What difference does it make how I feel about her?"

Marv stood up.

He said that it made quite a lot of difference. He had not, he reminded her, been in favor of Sue taking on this job. Since she had refused to take his advice, he felt very strongly that it would be to her advantage to make friends with Gloria, try to like her, to get along on an amicable basis. "Play it cool," he said.

Which, Sue recalled, was precisely the advice he had given Martha.

Why was he so determined to have everyone *play it cool* with that blonde?

What was behind it?

There was only one thing she could think of. Marv was fascinated by the woman, fascinated by her golden beauty, by her clever, knowing way of playing up to a man.

She said through gritted teeth: "I don't like her, and I have no intention of trying to like her. She can pull the wool over your eyes because you're a man." She interrupted herself to remark that she would never, never understand why men—otherwise intelligent, sane men—seemed to lose all their reasoning faculties where a gorgeous blonde was concerned.

"Obviously, Marv, you are completely unable to see her for what she is." She had deserted her husband seven years ago. Then, when she received the news that he had only a few months to live, back she came running, pretending she wanted to fill his remaining days with comfort and happiness.

"She's such an obvious phony," Sue said, and found Marv's hands suddenly on her arms. He was hurting her.

He was saying a thing so astonishing she could scarcely believe her own ears.

"Suppose we turn that around," he was saying. "How would you like me to question your motives?"

"What do you mean?"

"Can't you figure it out for yourself?" he asked, reminding her of a few incontrovertible facts.

"Who ran out on Dave only weeks before the date set for your wedding?"

Silently she stared at him.

"Who went away and left the poor guy's heart to break? *Why* did he go so crazy with grief that he tried to destroy himself drinking and playing around, and ended up marrying a girl he scarcely knew? Because he figured that might help him forget the other girl. Who was responsible for all that, my dear?"

Still she was silent.

His voice went on relentlessly. "And who was the girl who came rushing back after seven years to act as his nurse during his last days? It seems a little late in the day for that girl to come back, claiming she wants to give him what comfort and happiness she can."

His fierce dark eyes probed hers. "But she came. She's here. Why? Why should her motives be so noble and above suspicion? Or to put it another way—" he sounded angry—"who is to say this girl didn't have a tender, romantic, death-bed marriage in mind?"

Which, he pointed out, would have left her a wealthy widow.

Not wanting him to suspect how deeply his words hurt, Sue held back the angry protest which had parted her lips. Marv *knew* why she had broken off with Dave. He knew that *he* was the one to blame.

She turned away from him, her normally full, soft lips a tight, harsh line as she stared down at the fire.

"Now you're sore at me, aren't you?"

"Shut up!" She breathed deeply. Still staring at the leaping, dancing flames, her thoughts raced back to the night when they had walked in the moonlight, then had stopped walking. And Marv, his arms hard and insistent around her, had begged: "Tell Dave the truth about us. He'll be hurt, but he'll get over it. You and I belong together. You know we do sweetheart. Don't you know it?"

She had known it.

But she had also known she could never find happiness if she trampled over a man's heart to get what she wanted. And at the time Marv had believed that her decision was right, or had pretended to believe it.

"By the way, nursing must be hard work, isn't it?"

He put the question as casually as if her career had been the subject under discussion.

"In a way."

"Mother told me you had trained as a psychiatric nurse."

He wondered if that was correct, while Sue wondered how he dared question her about her work after his insulting remarks.

She had had enough psychiatric training, she told him, to deal with problem children; not specifically the seriously mentally disturbed, but border-line cases.

"I see. That must be interesting work."

"It is. Most interesting."

"But very hard work, I should think."

A silly conversation. "Yes. It is hard work," Sue agreed, her tone flat.

She had the impression that he was leading up to something. But she couldn't think what, until once again she felt his hands on her arms. He turned her around, standing still in front of her.

"Dealing with obstreperous, defiant, mixed up kids day after day, year after year—yes, I guess that would be devilish hard work. Very wearing." In fact, he thought it might put a girl under such a strain and tension that "she would resort to practically anything to escape from it."

He had a right to his own opinion, Sue said coldly. She didn't happen to feel that way about it. She liked children; she was said to be good at handling youngsters. When a hitherto sullen, difficult child suddenly responded with love and friendliness, it gave her a good feeling.

She said: "You feel needed."

"Sweet, understanding Sue." His smile was faintly amused. "Always one to think of others. An angel of mercy, so to speak, wearing a cap and uniform. That's my Sue."

Suddenly his smile was gone, giving way to

unexpected anger which threatened to get out of control. He began to walk up and down the small room, pushing his clenched fists in his pockets.

"That was the image you always showed to the world, wasn't it?

"Maybe you should have been an actress." He stopped squarely in front of her again. "How about that? Did you ever consider going on the stage?"

Sue laughed, but not with any humor. She was furious. She knew what he meant, even before he snapped: "Or how about trying for TV commercials, say advertising cosmetics that aren't worth a darn? With your syrupy voice and those big blue eyes, you could have persuaded millions of gullible dames to buy little jars filled with worthless goo. They'd swallow your lies about how the stuff would restore the bloom of youth to their wrinkled old hides. How could they not believe you? Your voice is so filled with sincerity."

Abruptly her hand shot out. It was the first time in her life she had ever slapped a man. "I'm sick of your insults. I've taken all of your snide, stupid insinuations I intend to take." Her voice was shrill.

"If you're in love with your brother's wife, that's your business." She drew a deep, difficult breath. Her eyes were blazing, all but shooting off fiery sparks as she added without thinking: "If this is a game to see who can shout the nastiest insults, how do I know you aren't playing hand in glove with Gloria?"

"Meaning?"

"Do you want me to draw a blueprint?" He was still a poor struggling lawyer. When Dave was gone, presumably dear, sweet Gloria would be a very rich widow. She could use a shrewd, knowledgeable lawyer to look after her money. "If the two of you arranged to marry, you'd be sitting pretty."

"You've got it all worked out, haven't you?"

His tone was amused. That served to enrage her still more. Having started toward the bedroom to get her dress, she turned back.

A few minutes ago, she reminded him, he had made a few high-sounding remarks about passing judgment on others. So what gave him the right to call *her* a phony?

"I did not call you a phony, my dear."

"I am not your dear, and don't try to deny what you just got through saying! What right have you to say that I'm fed up with my hospital work?

"To hear you talk, Marv Crowell, anyone would think I started out when I was practically in rompers to deceive the world as to my true nature."

This seemed to amuse him still more. He laughed aloud. Then, without warning, two long strides brought him close to her, and he took her in his arms.

Her breath seemed to stop.

One side of her mind was hating him for the things he had said, but her heart was not concerned with words. He was so tall, so strong. His eyes, those piercing dark eyes, were blazing into hers.

He said in an utterly changed tone, a soft, murmuring tone: "Don't you know when a man is being torn apart because he isn't sure what to believe? Can't you guess?"

She was silent, her eyes held in his.

He pulled her closer. "Has it never occurred to you that *another* man can carry the dream of a girl in his heart for years without end?"

Still she was silent, locked close in his arms.

His words came, little more than a whisper. "Sweet Sue." This time the words were like a caress. "Once, on a moonlit night, I discovered that I loved you. I still do."

When his dark head bent and his lips found hers, the ecstasy, the pounding of her heart were more than she could bear.

"Let me go," she cried, pulling away from him. She was frightened, frightened of the storm of feeling which tore through her like a tidal wave.

In less than ten minutes she was dressed, running back toward the big house as if she were pursued by a demon.

Chapter 8

To the side of the cottage sitting room was a flagstoned patio, flush with the ground. It had not been put there, complete with plastic awning, for the convenience of a scheming, jealous woman to see what she could see. But it did come in handy for that purpose.

Well, what do you know! said Gloria to herself as she peered through the French windows. She watched with interest the romantic scene in progress.

In one way she was extremely annoyed. What could Marv see in that nurse? She was no beauty, and obviously the type to fall into the arms of any man who happened to be handy. She would have expected Marv Crowell to be more discriminating.

Never once, she thought, had he made the slightest romantic gesture in *her* direction, although she had made it plain enough that she would not have responded with righteous indignation had he done so. Not that she would have gone along with any arrangement that might get her in hot water if it were discovered. She wasn't that stupid. There was too much at stake.

Still, a lot could be said between a man and a girl by subtle, lingering glances, or the touch of a hand when no one was looking, or even by the tone of a man's voice.

Marv hadn't said any of it to her. It was very frustrating.

But on the other hand, it just might be that this pretty little scene had provided her with a weapon she could use to good purpose.

Hidden from sight by the clump of shrubbery beside the cottage door, Gloria stood watching Sue take off like a rocket heading for the moon. She continued to stand thoughtfully for some moments debating how best to use this little weapon.

Meanwhile Marv too watched Sue rush off in the rain, which was now no more than a gentle drizzle. He went back into the cottage, stirred the fire and put on a fresh log. Then he pulled up a chair, relit his pipe, stared at the flames, and wondered if he had made the mistake of his life when, all those years ago, he had let Sue go out of his life.

There was no way of knowing if he could have overcome her objections, persuaded her that they had a right to their happiness in spite of Dave. But he could have tried.

He could have refused to be pushed aside, as if their suddenly found love were a wrong and despicable thing.

He could have followed her when she went East to train for nursing. He could have kept after her until her defenses were worn down.

That she had loved him in that long ago moment he had never doubted. He had seen the love in her eyes, had felt it as she yielded to his embrace, her arms around him telling him all that her lips refused to say. Telling him that she longed for his urgent lips against her own, then and forevermore. Telling him mutely all the secrets that mark a girl in love.

Maybe he could have persuaded her that their love was the most important thing in the world; maybe not. But he had never tried to find out.

He had made a point of never seeing her after that one memorable night. And even though she had touched a chord in him that no other girl ever had, he still had no regrets.

That he would do precisely as he had done—*just let her go*—even if he had to do over, he had no doubt. For now, as then, his feeling of responsibility for Dave had to come first, because of his promise to a dying man.

He got up to poke a crumbling log. He wondered what there was about an open fire which stirred memories in a man; memories perhaps best forgotten. He went to the kitchen, returned with a fresh drink, and sat thinking of Luke, the man who had been the dear, beloved friend of his boyhood as well as his stepfather.

It was Jake, the grandfather, the old man with the money, who had taken an unreasoning dislike to Marv. He had been an irascible, unloving old gentleman who imagined that everyone was after his fortune. Luke his son, had been a college professor of history; an impractical dreamer, in the old man's opinion. When Luke married Martha, a penniless widow with a three-year-old son, old Jake had stormed and raged, swearing that neither this fortune-hunting woman nor her child would ever get their hands on a cent of his money.

Luke, an understanding, compassionate man, was the one who had taken Marv to his heart. He had taken the boy fishing, taught him the exciting wonders to be found during a walk through the woods, talked to him as one adult to another, and on his death bed had asked the fifteen-year-old boy for one promise.

"Promise me you'll look after Dave as best you can. He's too much like me for his own good, sensitive, impractical, with too much charm."

Well, to sum up, Dave had every reason to believe he was a darling of the gods. His mother adored him and spoiled him. He was due to inherit most of his grandfather's fortune. He had everything going for him, except that there was no toughness in him. He was weak, because nothing had ever happened to him to help him develop strength.

"I'm scared for him, Marv, real scared." Life had a way of hitting hard at spoiled darlings, hitting in a way they least expected. And if Dave ever got hurt really badly, how would he take it? How could he stand up to a tough knockout blow?

"I've tried to be a friend to you, boy; tried to be

like a real father. So here's one thing you can do for me. Promise you'll do your best to keep Dave from getting hurt. And if something bad happens to him, stand by him. *Don't ever let him down. Promise?*"

Marv had promised.

And I've tried to keep that promise, he thought, sipping his drink, feeling mist in his eyes as he thought about Luke, the man who had been a friend to a lonely, troubled boy.

He was one swell guy and I loved him, Marv said aloud, and heard a knock on the door.

When he opened it and saw Gloria, his greeting was not one of bubbling enthusiasm. "Something you wanted?"

"Hi, you fascinating man."

"Hi."

"Aren't you going to invite me in, darling?"

She came in, looking gorgeous as usual, her slender, long-legged body swathed in a leopard-skin robe. Studying her as she sank gracefully into an easy chair, Marv wondered what there was about the woman that made his skin prickle. He couldn't stand the sight of her.

Could she please have a martini? she asked, helping herself to a cigarette from the brass box on the cocktail table.

Then she decided she would like some crackers and cheese. She was absolutely ravenous. Who wouldn't be, after going without her dinner? "That's why I phoned you, Marv. I wanted you to take me somewhere for a steak, plus some champagne and dreamy music. I needed to be cheered up."

Of course, had she realized he was entertaining that plain-looking, anything but attractive nurse —"Whatever do you see in that girl, Marv?"

He brought in a plate stacked with crackers and three varieties of cheese. "Help yourself," he said, and sat down.

Gloria nibbled daintily at one cracker, then decided that was all she wanted to eat. What she really wanted was company, someone to talk to, to make her come alive.

She had had a ghastly day. She hardly knew how she had survived it and lived to tell the tale.

First that impossible nurse had arrived. Imagine how it had made her feel to walk into the room to find this creature clasped in her husband's arms, like a long lost sister.

"I'm sure that's the way he feels about her," Marv said calmly, reaching for his pipe.

"Ha!" Still, Gloria had not made a scene. After all, Dave, being so ill and all, was more to be pitied than blamed.

Then, without any warning, at all, he had had the most awful spell. "He just fainted away. I was sure he was dying right before my eyes." She had nearly died herself, she was so scared.

Later, of course, he had revived. She had gone to her room to rest and get over the shock. Then she had gone out for a drive.

But it seemed to be one of those days. No matter

what she did, something went wrong. Finally she ended up at the Blue Tavern, where she ran into an old friend from Hollywood. He was a nice enough guy, except that when he drank he had a compulsion to tell the sad story of his life to whomever he happened to be talking to.

"So I was stuck with him." She explained she had a kind heart and hated to hurt anyone's feelings. Well, one sad story led to another. This fellow, Chuck by name, dreamed up stories as he went along. By the time she escaped, the rain was pouring and the highway was as slippery as glass.

"That was the reason I phoned you, Marv. I wanted you to come and drive me home. I'm absolutely terrified of driving the Jag in the rain."

"Thought you said you wanted me to buy you a dinner?"

Well, anyway, she had managed to get safely back to the house. "And it was like walking into a tomb."

Dave was in a deep sleep. No sound from his room.

No sound from Martha's room.

No sound, period, except that very suddenly there was a strange sound inside the wall in her room, as if somebody were tapping.

"Do you suppose the house could be haunted, Marv?" she asked, adding that she was simply terrified of the very thought of spooks.

"Probably a mouse in the wall," Marv suggested. He added that there had been a little trouble of that sort about a year ago.

"Oh, good heavens!"

"Let's turn on the TV," Marv suggested presently. "Help you get your mind off your troubles." He got up and found a program featuring a much publicized clairvoyant who, purportedly, could give the most amazing prophecies.

As the picture came on, the tall, dark young man was saying: "I do not claim to be one hundred percent right in my predictions."

He could, however, claim close to eighty percent accuracy, a far better average than could fairly be attributed to chance, especially when you considered the fact that his information came to him in pictures; in symbols, so to speak. Then he had to translate these symbols into terms expressing their actual meaning.

"Would you explain," the M.C. asked, "how these pictures come to you?" Did he just see them in the air?

No. "I take this crystal ball." The tall young man picked up a glass ball from the table before him. "And after I gaze intently into it for a few minutes—"

"Turn that devilish thing off!"

It was a shriek shrill with rage as Gloria jumped to her feet and rushed across the room. She pushed the off knob with such force that the jade lady on top of the set toppled over.

"Have you gone nuts?" Marv sounded angry as he set the figurine back in place. That jade piece happened to be one of his most prized possessions.

"I don't happen to care for TV," Gloria said coldly. She sat down again, finished her drink and lit a cigarette. But she was breathing hard, and something close to terror was written on her face.

Marv stared at her thoughtfully and found himself wondering, not for the first time, if the beauteous Gloria was a psycho.

Chapter 9

After Marv had watched Gloria for some minutes, studying that carefully made up face, wondering exactly why she had come there tonight and what she was after, he glanced at his watch. He stood up, his back to the fire.

He said: "Frankly, Gloria, I'll have to ask you to continue this visit some other time." He spoke of being due in court at ten in the morning. He was to plead an important case, and he needed a good night's sleep.

"Sit down," she said curtly. There was an issue to be settled between them tonight. "You see," she went on firmly, "Dave might die at any minute." Therefore it was imperative that he make out a will without more delay.

"His son's interests must be protected," she said with all the passionate intensity of a doting mother who would rather be burned at the stake than allow her beloved child to be robbed of all he should inherit.

Marv decided the fire could use a fresh log. He put one on. If she was about to lay her cards on the table, their discussion could last far into the night.

He was surprised at her sudden direct approach. It was not the first time she had mentioned the will, but before she had been considerably more subtle in her remarks.

That TV program seemed to have had some strange effect on the girl.

She announced flatly: "I am bringing Bobby here tomorrow. The sooner Dave gets to know his son, the better. After that—well, it's up to you. As a lawyer, I trust you to handle Bobby's interests properly."

Hands in his pockets, he strode about the room for a moment, looking lost in thought.

"Exactly where is the kid?" he asked presently.

Her pretty mouth, usually shaped like a kiss, set in a tight, determined line. "I've told you, Marv. He is in a place for—well, problem children."

"He's a mental case?"

"Of course not." She was shouting. There was nothing mentally wrong with Bobby. It was just that she had so little time to give him, plus the fact that he had no father image to hold to. All in all, the boy no doubt suffered from a deep feeling of insecurity. That undoubtedly was the reason he had become so imaginative, made up stories that weren't true. She sighed deeply, her tone suddenly soft and sad. That was why it had seemed best to put him in this home.

There was, she added, a very fine woman in charge, a Mrs. Thompson, who was very motherly and loving. She was truly gifted at handling youngsters who were slightly mixed up. And she took a special interest in Bobby. She said he reminded her of the little six-year-old son she had lost years ago.

As she told all this, Gloria's mouth resumed its practiced smile.

Then back came the tight, angry scowl when Marv inquired pleasantly: "Are you saying the kid is a liar?"

"I said he was very imaginative." She supposed it was what the experts called psychopathic lying, which was quite a different thing, in her opinion, from *real* lying.

"How different?"

"Oh, for heaven's sakes." She got to her feet, thoroughly irritated. "What's the idea of putting me through the third degree?"

Bobby needed to know his father. That was what it all got down to. He needed a father's love before it was too late.

"Most of all he needs his dad's dough. Right?"

She stood directly in front of him, her mouth working before she said: "Have it your own way. Then answer this one question. Since he is Dave's son, why shouldn't he inherit his father's money?"

Marv went through the motions of considering that question. "Okay. After the happy reunion takes place, I'll advise Dave to set up a trust fund for little Bobby. That can be worked out easily."

"No!"

Gloria wanted no part of any trust fund. For one

thing, as often as not trust companies were run by crooks. Once they got control of a person's money, they resorted to all sorts of schemes to help themselves to what didn't belong to them.

"I am the best one to handle the money."

Therefore Dave's will must be made out, naming her as beneficiary, not only because of the boy, but because—

"You can stop right there," Marv cut in. "You were about to say you had your rights, as Dave's legal wife."

"Of course."

"Has it occurred to you, Gloria, that you are the one who deserted your husband, that you refused to live with him as his wife? So what gives you the idea that you have any legal rights?"

The look she gave him was one of unvarnished hatred. She bit hard on her underlip, then reached for a cigarette which she fitted into the holder and lit before she burst out savagely: "This conversation is getting nowhere fast, so let's skip it."

She inhaled smoke, then blew it squarely in his face. "Let's get down to brass tacks, friend."

She wanted Dave's will made out in her favor. "And if you refuse to play along, you'll be sorry."

He reminded her, his voice pleasant, that it was neither his money nor his will.

"True," she agreed. "But Dave has every confidence in you. He thinks you're clever, honest, and the salt of the earth. And since the guy is too sick and weak to make decisions for himself, he'll take your advice on how he should dispose of his money."

And, she snapped, she didn't want to hear any eyewash about what Marv happened to believe was right and ethical. She couldn't care less about the ethics of the matter.

Her face close up to his, she rushed on: "I want that money! I'm sick of being poor, sick of struggling to get a foothold in lousy show business. And all for what? If I ever do get anywhere, it will be when I'm too old to enjoy the things I want when I get them.

"I want things now! I want diamonds and furs and a posh penthouse apartment where I can look out over the world and spit on it if I feel like it. I want money, money, money. I've always wanted money more than anything on earth, lots of it. Other women want love, or a career, or to do good to others. I want money, and this is my one chance to get it, and *you are going to help me get it*. Is that clear?"

Her mouth worked, her face looked contorted, her eyes blazed. Watching her, Marv shuddered deep inside.

As a lawyer, he had come in contact with avaricious women. But this was the first time he had ever stared into the eyes of a woman who was obsessed by greed.

She looked demented.

He realized that it would be futile to reason with her, or attempt to explain legal technicalities, or tell her that to exert undo influence over Dave would be highly unethical.

Gloria was in no mood to listen to any remarks about such trivial matters as legalities or ethics.

In fact, she did not care to listen to anything he had to say about anything.

"I mean every word I'm saying, and you'd better believe me."

He had better agree right there and then to start putting pressure on Dave, to get the will down in writing, signed and witnessed.

Not that she would be unreasonable in her demands. Naturally, it would take some days, possibly a week or so, for Dave to get used to the idea that he actually had a son.

Sick people sometimes became stubborn. If they got the notion that their loved ones couldn't wait for them to die, they had to be handled with tact and diplomacy. It was aggravating having to be patient with them. You had to grit your teeth and pretend to have the patience of Job.

"But it isn't too soon for you to start working on him, Marv. You should know best how to poke and prod at him, how to drum into his poor, sick mind that he should write exactly the kind of will I want written."

Suddenly she was all smiling sweetness. "So get with it, sweetie. Understand?"

"I understand what you're saying, yes. But suppose I decide he should divide the estate between his mother and various charities and advise him to do just that?"

"You could do that, of course." She was still smiling. "But if you do—" She shrugged, killed her cigarette, and told him: "I, too, have a sense of duty, my dear man. And I'm afraid I might feel it my duty to tell poor Dave what I witnessed in this room tonight, and what I overheard while I stood outside in the rain."

He looked amused. "So you were spying." So what? Whatever she had seen or heard, there was nothing shameful or in any sense terrible; merely two old friends meeting and showing a little affection after a long separation.

Walking toward the door, she threw him a smile over her shoulder; a smile which held a sordid, deadly threat.

"Sweetie, when I tell my little story, it will add up to more, much more, than an innocent little visit between two dear old friends."

"Yeah?"

She turned back to tell him: "It will be a meeting between a scheming nurse and a critically ill man's brother. The two were sweethearts in the long, long ago. The nurse was explaining that she came rushing back, expecting to marry my poor, dear, unsuspecting husband on his death bed, so that she could get his money, then marry you when he was gone. What will it do to poor Dave when I tell him all this, and his pitiful romantic dream is blasted to kingdom come?"

She asked gently: "You wouldn't want to do that to the poor guy, would you?"

"You'd be lying."

"Really?" Oh, she'd probably be giving what she had overheard a few twists and turns. "But do you deny accusing dear, sweet Sue of being a designing nurse who had a death bed marriage in mind?"

Before he could digest that threat, Gloria reverted to the beauteous, throaty-voiced, appealing creature who she imagined to be irresistible.

Moving close, she brought her soft, beautiful hands to his shoulders. "I don't want to fight with you, Marv. You see, I'm in love with you and—oh, I might as well be honest. I was eaten up with jealousy when I discovered that nurse here with you."

Pulling her hands from his shoulders, he said roughly: "Look, Gloria, don't try trick or treat with me."

She shook her head sadly. "I'm not playing a game. I'm in deadly earnest. Would you believe me if I said you are the one and only man who has ever attracted me seriously?"

"No."

"But it's true."

He laughed aloud. "Well, don't let it worry you. You'll get over it."

"I can't help thinking how wonderful life could be for both of us, darling, after poor Dave is gone.

Think what fun we could have with all that money."

"You think about it, dear. As I said, I'm not interested in trick or treat."

She gave him an offended glare. Her parting words were not exactly polite, and after she was gone Marv stood before the fire for a long while. His eyes were troubled.

For probably the one and only time in his life he was a frightened man, frightened for Susan.

He couldn't figure in exactly what way this money-greedy woman could hurt Susan. That was what bothered him. It was like a court trial. When you couldn't figure your opponent's next move ahead of time, it was very disturbing. Anything could happen.

She's a bad one, this Gloria, he decided grimly, and went to bed.

Chapter 10

The next day the sun shone. The ocean, skirting the highway, looked like a calm, shimmering lake. And Gloria, driving south in the Jaguar, wore a serene smile on her beautiful face.

She wore blue shorts; a blue cashmere sweater was draped over her shoulders. A blue scarf bound her pale hair.

The boy on the seat beside her also wore blue shorts and a matching pullover sweater. She had thought it would be nice for mother and son to wear matching color schemes.

Bobby was a sturdy little boy with unruly black hair and rather fierce dark eyes. As they drove along, he scowled glumly ahead through the windshield. His general expression was one of defiance.

He spoke when he was spoken to—if he cared to, not otherwise. Which Gloria found very frustrating. They had left Los Angeles around noon. It was now close to two o'clock, and during all those hundred miles of driving it had been impossible to conduct a loving mother-and-son conversation with Bobby.

She had tried. Heaven knows she had tried.

But all she could get out of him was "No," or "Yeah," or "I want an ice cream cone."

She was at her wits' end. Maybe she should have done some homework on child psychology, or been born with an extra shot of maternal instinct.

Maybe he's scared, she thought suddenly. That seemed logical. The boy was being taken to meet the father he had never seen. That would be a traumatic experience for any child who had never known his daddy. Naturally, it would get him all confused and upset, and, child-like, he would give all the signs of going into a tantrum.

When they were less than ten miles from Hillcrest, Gloria parked the car by the side of the highway. "Now, darling," she said, "you and I must have a little talk."

"About what?"

"Oh," she smiled, "let's call it a dress rehearsal." She opened her bag. "Want a chocolate bar, honey?"

"No," said Bobby, announcing that he hated chocolate.

"Since when?" Gloria asked, reminding him that he should mind his manners.

"Say, 'no thank you, Mummy dear.'"

"Go climb a tree," said Bobby.

Gloria tensed. She longed passionately to slap that glowering, impudent little face. No wonder some mothers went completely berserk and ended up in a lunatic asylum. The ones who retained their sanity, how did they stand it, cooped up day after day, year after year, with anywhere from one to a dozen of the little savages?

Her voice was sweet and loving. "Now listen to me, sweetie. We're almost there. In less than half an hour you'll be meeting the father you've never seen."

"I don't want to see the old guy."

"Bobby!" What way was that to talk? For one thing, his daddy wasn't old. He was just a bit over thirty.

"That's old." When he got to be thirty, said Bobby, delivering his first lengthy remark, he was going to shoot himself.

"That's silly talk," smiled Gloria, determined to make a joke of the child's idiotic chatter.

"You talk silly, too," said Bobby. "Some of your silly talk makes me want to throw up."

"Oh, shut up." Gloria's temper was struggling to get out of hand. Her hand came down, not too gently, on a cringing shoulder.

"Keep your mouth shut, and listen to what I'm saying. Your daddy is a very sick man. That's the first thing for you to remember."

She paused, getting a cigarette from her bag. She simply must not let her poor shot nerves get the best of her, must not let the provoking child see that he was getting the upper hand. That was axiomatic, wasn't it?

She smoked thoughtfully for a moment, then continued. "Now, when I take you in to meet your daddy, I think it would please him if you called him 'Darling Daddy' and threw your arms around him. Will you do that, Bobby?"

"No."

"Why not, dear?"

"Because he's just a strange guy I never saw in my life. Why should I get mushy over him?"

"It's not his fault you never saw him, honey. You see he—well, he didn't know he had a son. Now that he does know, he'll be all choked up with love at the very sight of you."

"Hogwash."

"Bobby! I want you to stop those vulgar, impudent remarks." She was taking him to a very grand home where he would be received as a beloved son. The least he could do when he got there was to behave like a little gentleman.

Bobby grimaced, announcing that he was not a little gentleman. He was a little roughneck and a liar to boot. That's what Old Lady Thompson said he was, and she ought to know.

Choosing to disregard this comment, Gloria went on with practiced sweetness. "And I want you to treat me with the courtesy a loving mother is entitled to." Perhaps, she conceded, it was impossible for him to feel any deep love for her. After all, it seemed to have gone out of style for children these days to love and respect their parents.

"I don't love you," announced Bobby. "I don't even like you."

"What don't you like about me?" Gloria asked

sweetly, her patience strained.

"I don't like all the goo you put on your face. And I don't like you touching me. And I don't like—" Bobby gave a deep, long-drawn-out sigh—"oh, just about everything."

Gloria leaned toward him. "Young man, I've had just about enough of your stupid, idiotic, childish impudence. How you feel about me doesn't make any real difference. Even if you hate me—"

Well, he wouldn't be the first child to hate his own mother. If that was the way he felt, he must conceal his feelings.

"You ain't my mother," said Bobby, adding that his real mother had gone away to heaven. She was young and beautiful, and she didn't have any smelly old goo on her face.

"Listen, sweetie, you must stop believing that childish lie." A lot of youngsters, she explained patiently, dreamed up a make-believe mother. When their real mama didn't have much time for them, or didn't suit them for one reason or another, they sort of invented a mother more to their liking. But she wasn't real. She was just a dream, and all right for very little kids to imagine.

"But you're a big boy now, Bobby. And I'm your real mother who loves you very much." She turned away to tap off her cigarette ash, discard the stub, and turned back just in time to catch the red tip of a pointed little tongue thrust in her direction.

That did it.

She grabbed his shoulders hard. When he howled furiously: "Take your hands off me," she slapped his face, and snapped, out of the rage boiling up inside her: "I'd like to kill you, you little brat. If you don't behave yourself, *maybe I will*."

Watching her with the wary, speculative eyes of a trapped animal, Bobby huddled at the far side of the seat.

"Now," she said more calmly, "are you going to do as you're told?"

"Maybe."

Watching him, studying that defiant, closed face, Gloria hoped that she hadn't gone too far. "Well, here we go," she said brightly, heading the Jag back to the highway. She drove with more caution than she usually did, because she was thinking hard. It was silly to regard this child as a dangerous enemy, to be afraid of him. But with so much at stake, she was scared.

Me and my temper, she thought. She'd have to watch it.

Chapter 11

Sue awoke that same morning feeling refreshed, revitalized, ready to cope with any and all problems. This was surprising. She had expected to face the day with all the energy and enthusiasm of a tattered rag. But somehow, before she slept, she had come to terms with herself.

She was there; she had taken on certain responsibilities simply by coming. Now it was up to her to accept those responsibilities, such as doing her best to be a loving, kind, compassionate companion for Dave. Unhappily, this seemed about all she could do for him.

Leukemia must inevitably run its course. There was little anyone could do except wait. In some cases, of course, the patient lived for quite a few years, but not always. Poor Dave. Her heart ached, thinking how he had changed. The laughing, joyous, handsome, carefree Dave she had once known and imagined she loved seemed already gone.

Still lying in bed, she thought of something an elderly doctor had once told her. "Death can be a sweeter, more pleasant experience than most people realize." Too much morbid horror had been built up around the idea of death. That was all wrong. Actually, it could be an easier experience than birth; just a gentle, peaceful loss of consciousness. That was the way nature intended it to be.

Sue said a little prayer, asking that it might be that way for Dave. Then she got up, and decided while she was showering that she would try to get along with Gloria as best she could. It's not up to me, she thought, to pass judgment on her or question her intentions.

And as for Marv—forget him!

Sitting before the mirror as she brushed her hair, she informed herself that her adolescent dream of the man was simply a hangup from years ago. She should have gotten rid of it long since.

He's trying to use you for some reason or other, she told the mirror.

Man, the manipulator.

That summed up Marv Crowell. It explained his protestation of love last night.

Myrtle, the little maid, was leaving. "I've decided I don't care for cleaning and hustling trays for sick people," she announced when Sue went down to the kitchen for coffee. And now that Mrs. Harding was bringing a brat into the house—

"When she gets back, tell her the cook and I decided to pack and get out."

"Mrs. Harding has gone out?" Sue was surprised. She wouldn't have taken Gloria for the type to be up with the birds.

"Yeah. Old Mrs. Harding too." Ever since she had taken this job, said Myrtle, the old woman had been ailing. Now it seemed she wasn't ailing any more. She had taken off in her car, spry as you please. "Said to look for her when you saw her."

What do you know? thought Sue, and finished her second cup of coffee before she hurried back upstairs to see how Dave was doing.

To her surprise, Dave too seemed to have taken a new lease on life. He was up and out on the sun deck adjoining his room. His color was better, his eyes seemed brighter. When he spoke, saying among other things how pretty she looked in her uniform, there was more life in his voice.

"I'd like some wheat cakes," he informed her, "with maple syrup and very thin slices of ham. And an omelette."

"You were planning to chop down a few trees after breakfast?" Sue grinned, wondering if it really was her arrival that made him seem a little like his old, youthful self.

He said that it was. "I dreamed about you last night," he told her. He had dreamed that she was right there in the house with him. Then when he woke up and realized it was for real, he couldn't wait to get up and start the day.

By the time Sue went downstairs again both Myrtle and the cook had taken their departure.

Sue fixed the breakfast herself, taking two trays upstairs so that she could eat with Dave.

Not until they had finished did Dave mention the expected arrival of the boy he had never heard of until a few weeks ago. Last night—it must have been around midnight or later—Gloria had waked him to tell him to brace himself. He was to meet his son today.

"How do you feel about it, Dave?"

"You mean about seeing the boy?" To be honest, he didn't feel much of anything.

After a moment of thought he added: "I am a bit curious to see the youngster." He hoped he wouldn't do or say the wrong thing. He also hoped the boy wasn't expecting a rousing, dramatic scene. That he definitely was not up to.

It was around three in the afternoon when Gloria drove into the carport, then came dancing up the stairs, calling as she came: "Get ready, darling. Here we come."

After a quiet day spent reading and resting, Dave was sitting at a card table drawn up to the window. Sue was across from him. She had just let him beat her at a game of rummy.

"Now don't go all to pieces, sweetie." Tripping across the room, Gloria put a loving arm around Dave, said she knew how excited he must be, but—doctor's orders—he simply must not get overly excited.

Then, beckoning to the boy who stood in the doorway: "Come here, sweetheart. It's high time you and your daddy got to know each other. Come here, I say!" The syrupy voice sharpened a trifle. "Don't just stand there."

With obvious reluctance, Bobby scowled his way across to where Dave sat watching him with considerable interest.

Sue was interested, too. Six years old? she mused. The boy was certainly big for his age.

"Hi, Bobby." Dave extended his hand—to the empty air.

"Hi," Bobby said, fingers thrust firmly under the belt of his shorts.

"Sweetheart, shake hands with your daddy," ordered Gloria. "And do take that frown off your face, pet."

"I don't feel like shaking hands," Bobby announced, adding: "I ain't supposed to shake hands with strangers. Old Lady Thompson said I shouldn't. I might catch a germ or something."

"You're quite right." Dave grinned amiably, then suggested that Bobby say hello to his pretty nurse. "Her name is Susan, but we call her Sue. And if you should catch any germs, she'll take good care of you."

Bobby turned his scowling countenance toward Sue, who was saying casually: "Hi, pal. Would you like an ice cream cone?"

"Yeah." For the first time the boy's set lips relaxed in the trace of a smile. "Chocolate."

"Bobby darling," interrupted Gloria, "you told me you hated chocolate. And furthermore, you've already had enough ice cream to kill a mule."

Her glance flicked over Sue. "I do not encourage him eating sweet stuff between meals."

"You ain't got nothing to do with my eating," said Bobby, all scowls again.

"And besides," continued Gloria, "I want my son to have a little loving, heart-to-heart talk with his father. So suppose you leave us alone for now, Nurse."

"Suppose you take yourself off, too, Gloria." Dave spoke pleasantly, his tone surprisingly firm. "Go somewhere and do whatever it is you do to your face when you can't think of anything else to do."

The color that showed above her makeup was the flush of rage. "I happen to be his mother, Dave. I think these are precious moments which the three of us should share."

Dave made it clear that he did not agree. He said with a smile, somewhat inelegantly: "Scram, baby."

He said: "This boy and I want to have a little man-to-man talk. We don't need any female chaperons. Right, Bobby?"

"Right." Bobby sounded, for Bobby, downright friendly. For good measure he added: "Maybe you ain't such a bad guy after all."

"What did you expect?" Dave asked. "A horn-tailed monster?"

With a shrug of his sturdy little shoulders, the boy said: "A kid like me never knows what to expect." He was scowling again, but not at Dave.

His scowl was directed meaningfully at the beautiful blonde woman who was concealing her anger and a touch of fear behind her customary practiced smile.

"Well, have fun, you two." And after a light kiss bestowed on Dave's cheek, she followed Sue from the room.

Chapter 12

After she had done over her hair, put on fresh makeup and changed to pink woolen pants and a pink blouse sparkling with crystals, Gloria decided that she was about to go out of her mind.

Tiptoeing along the hall, she put her ear to Dave's door. Not a sound. No talk, no whispered confidences between father and son. What were those two up to? were they holding a Quaker meeting of silence?

Eaten by curiosity, she opened the door noiselessly just a trifle. A chess board was set up on the card table.

Dave was teaching the child to play chess!

Back in her room, Gloria smoked three cigarettes, gazed for some moments at the mirror, thought fleetingly of Marv and their talk of last night.

Just to be on the safe side she should see Marv as soon as possible, make sure she hadn't lost any ground with him by telling the guy she was in love with him.

She was, of course. But some men were frightened when you mentioned the word *love*.

She went down to the kitchen and couldn't

believe her own eyes. Martha, according to plan, should have been in her room resting.

"What do you think you're doing?" demanded Gloria, deliberately ignoring Sue, who was at the sink scraping carrots. She made it a point to ignore the nurse whenever possible. How she detested that sweet, angelic, mealy-mouthed little hypocrite.

"It should be obvious what I'm doing," said Martha who was at the work table arranging steaks she had taken from the freezer. But in case it was not—

"I'm taking charge in my own kitchen, in my own home." Her hair was beautifully coiffed, she wore a new becoming print dress, and she looked at least ten years younger than she'd been looking these last few weeks.

"If you have any objection, Gloria, I suggest that you take it up with my lawyer in San Diego. Belmont is his name. Sam Belmont. He was a friend of Luke, my deceased husband, God rest his soul."

And so, said Martha, sprinkling a bit of tenderizer over the steaks, she had decided to drive in to have a little talk with Sam.

"He told me that you had no right to take over in my home. He said you must have gotten that court order by persuading some crooked lawyer to tell the court a pack of lies. My darling Dave may be an ill man, but he is not mentally sick. So it's up to him to sign any papers, saying who he wants to take charge of his affairs. That's what Sam said."

"Some old creep," sneered Gloria.

"Oh, Sam isn't as young as he once was," Martha conceded sweetly. "But he was a Federal judge for many years." So she guessed he knew what he was talking about.

Moving with all the agility and the grace of a girl, Martha got out the broiler pan and greased it deftly before placing the steaks. "He said I was to go about my home as usual, running things to suit myself."

So now, since that trashy pair Gloria had brought in had skipped out, and good riddance, she was fixing a nice dinner.

"Sue, darling, there are some tomatoes to go with the salad." Not that they tasted the way tomatoes were supposed to taste. They had no taste at all, in fact. But they looked nice.

"And if you have any objections, Gloria, just go see my lawyer." That was another thing Sam had told her. She was not to engage in any arguments or discussion of the matter. "He said for me to keep my mouth shut. He would explain any fine points you wanted explained."

Ready to explode with frustration and rage, Gloria drew several deep breaths, threatened darkly to see this old guy and tell him what was what. Then she left the kitchen, hands clenched, and shaking with inward fury and righteous indignation.

Of course she was in the right. She was Dave's wife, wasn't she?

A wife had the right to run things in her husband's home, hadn't she?

And another thing: whatever had possessed old Martha suddenly to take things in her own hands? Until today she had been as meek as you please.

Was it possible that detestable Sue had hypnotized Martha? Of course it was possible. Nurses learned all sorts of tricks from their doctor pals. It was not unlikely that the girl had gotten control of the old woman's mind, was *willing* her to show some spunk and independence, *willing* her to rush off to see this lawyer.

Gloria rushed outdoors into the deepening dark. Maybe some fresh air would help to calm her down.

Inwardly she was seething. That awful nurse!

"Hello, Beautiful."

Engrossed in the turmoil of her thoughts, she was in front of Marv's cottage before she saw him coming around from the carport. She brightened, her lips parted in an entrancing smile. "Marv!"

Her voice was happy, as if he were a loved one she hadn't seen for a thousand years. "Can I come in for a drink?"

Nope. Giving her shoulder a friendly pat, he explained that this was the end of a long hard day. He needed to take a shower and to relax—and not in the company of a beautiful blonde.

"Oh, Marv." She pouted prettily. "Couldn't you put up with me for just a few minutes?"

He could, but he wasn't going to. "Has the son arrived?"

"Oh, yes." Dear little Bobby. Such a darling child. But a problem, too. She had so many many problems. They were driving her half out of her mind.

"Let me know when you're all the way out, dear."

"You brute." Her tone made the words a caress. "Marv?"

"Yes?"

"You aren't sore at me?"

"About what? "

"Oh, some of the things I said last night." After one too many martinis, she explained, very often she said things she later wished she hadn't.

"Who doesn't?" Anyway, he had already forgotten most of what she had said.

She looked at him thoughtfully. "I hope you haven't forgotten what I said about the will, and the things I want you to say to Dave."

He shook his head. No, he more or less recalled that part.

"Have you thought about it?"

"Yes."

"Well, have you come to a decision?"

"No, dear. I'm still thinking."

"How long do you expect to be thinking?"

"Until I come to a decision."

"Oh, you!"

Her voice took on a sudden intensity. "Listen, Marv, I simply must talk to you. For one thing, I'm getting a little tired of the way that nurse is trying to run things. I don't think she—well—" She hesitated. "I have reason to believe she's a disturbing influence."

"You mean Sue?" He laughed. Ridiculous. Sue wouldn't disturb a poor little mouse, if she could help it.

"I'm serious, Marv. Something very strange happened today, with your mother. She's isn't like herself."

"You don't say?" He sounded amused. "Don't tell me Ma has taken up Yoga exercises, like say standing on her head."

"This is nothing to joke about." Suddenly she was emphatic. "I've got to talk with you. If you don't want me to come here, then meet me at the Blue Tavern around nine o'clock."

Without another word, she left him and walked back to the big house.

Chapter 13

Sue was tempted to scream: "Oh, sit down, Gloria. Eat your dinner and shut up. Stop reminding Dave that he's at death's door. And do stop billing and cooing over Bobby. Can't you see the kid isn't buying your phony bill of motherly devotion?"

Naturally, she said none of it. But she couldn't altogether control her riotous, indignant thoughts. Why couldn't beautiful, glamorous Gloria have stayed away until dinner was over?

Everything had been so peaceful, so nice, until she came, her pink blouse throwing off glitter and sparkles, her personality projecting vibrations that upset everyone at the table.

"If you want steak," Martha said pleasantly, "you'll have to broil one for yourself. I didn't know when you were coming."

She smiled inwardly. She was finding Martha's astonishing change of front a joy and delight. Now she was like her old self, and she gave all the credit to Sue.

"I've been like somebody who was hit over the head with a heavy blunt instrument." she had confided while they were putting the finishing touches to dinner.

Gloria's arrival in itself had been a shock. "I just couldn't seem to get my bearings." Poor Dave was so ill, and she was so worried about him. Then there was all this threatening talk about a court order and sending her away, as if she had no rights in the home where she'd lived from the day Luke had brought her there as a bride.

"I felt so alone, Sue."

But after Sue came, she knew she wasn't alone any more. "You're young and smart and *loyal*. I knew you wouldn't let that person put anything over on me."

So all in all, she had gotten up that morning full of vigor and fight. After that it was as if she had been guided every step of the way the whole livelong day: into the city to talk with Sam, the lawyer; then to her doctor, who gave her a stiff shot of Vitamin 12, advised her to eat lots of proteins, visit the beauty shop to cheer herself up, and think kindly thoughts about everyone to keep her mind peaceful and calm.

All excellent advice, commented Sue, arranging celery hearts in a dish with olives and pickles. "See that you follow it, darling." To which Martha retorted that she would do her best.

"But I'm only human. So I hope God will understand why I find it next to impossible to think kindly thoughts about that woman."

Slipping her those codeine pills!

"We aren't *sure* they were doped, Martha."

"No? Maybe *you* aren't sure," said Martha darkly, and went into the dining room to light the candles on the table, which was set with her best silver and crystal.

After Dave said he felt up to coming downstairs to dinner, Martha had insisted on making it a special celebration. "With all the trimmings," she said.

The table did look beautiful, and for the first ten minutes or so things went beautifully. Dave seemed tired, as was to be expected, but he looked pleased and happy. And obviously he had established a good, friendly relationship with Bobby, who announced that Dave was his big brother.

Apparently finding everything to his liking, including Martha's hot biscuits (which he was pushing into his mouth with startling rapidity), Bobby seemed to be learning how to smile. He even giggled once or twice, the first time when Martha instructed him to address her as Marty.

"That's a funny name for an old lady like you."

At that point Gloria came strolling in. She seemed about to apologize sweetly for being late, then thought better of it as she glanced disapprovingly at the pretty candlelit table.

What was the big idea? she wanted to know, of all this fussing, setting the dining room table? Since this was a house of sickness, the sensible thing would be to eat in the kitchen alcove. Glancing irately at the woman who was, after a manner of speaking, her mother-in-law, Gloria snapped: "I suppose you're responsible for all this preposterous nonsense."

"If you want to eat," Martha said placidly, "sit down and eat." If she wanted a steak, she could go and get one. If not—"I won't have arguments at the table, Gloria." Arguing, she pointed out, was bad for the digestion. It spoiled everyone's appetite.

"You tell her, Marty," piped Bobby. "She spoils everything."

"How dare you!" Gloria began, then bit down hard on her underlip before she went on in her practiced syrupy voice: "Darling, my little sweetie, how can you say such a thing after all I've done for you?"

"Lemme alone," scowled Bobby. The child was seated to the right of Dave. As Gloria went to stand between them, she thought what a lovely picture she must present and wished it could be on TV—Daddy, Mummy, and Junior, she with one arm draped around each of "her men."

Bobby immediately ruined the effect by giving her a push with his elbow. "Don't touch me," he muttered. And just to prove that she was a woman of patience and strong will, Gloria did not box his ears as she longed passionately to do.

Instead, she turned her anger on Sue, who had gotten up to bring Dave a fresh glass of water. "What kind of nurse are you?" she demanded.

As she understood it, Sue had come there to serve as Dave's nurse during the days or weeks or whatever he had left.

It was right then that Sue felt the urge to scream out long and loud, and did not. Her lips firmly closed, her face blank of all expression, she brought Dave the water, poured a little more red wine in his crystal glass, and set her mind to doing the multiplication table while Gloria's harsh voice ranted on.

She's really losing her grip, thought Sue, deciding that Gloria sounded for all the world as if she were cracking up. Obviously she was wearing the mask of a devoted wife and mother. But the mask kept slipping.

"If you're a trained nurse as you claim to be, young lady, you should have sense enough to know that my poor beloved husband should be in his bed, resting."

What gave her the idea that a terminally ill man had the strength to come downstairs to eat, to drink and take part in all this other nonsense? Didn't she understand Dave must not become excited, that he must conserve his strength?

Gloria realized that she was losing control, but she couldn't call a halt to the furious rush of words that sprang to her lips. It had been too much for her to take, walking in here where they were all having such a fine, enjoyable time. All of her spleen and sense of outrage focused on Sue as she snapped: "You aren't fit to call yourself a nurse. You're doing my husband more harm than good, and I want you to get out of this house tonight. You're fired."

Calmly Sue replied: "I must remind you, Gloria, that you weren't the one who hired me. So I honestly don't understand how you can fire me."

"Pay her no mind," said Martha, just as Dave stood up, looking suddenly very tired.

"Shut your foolish mouth, Gloria," he said quietly, and turned to Sue, his eyes filled with sadness and love. "I'm sorry I brought you into this mess, honey. But now that you're here—*please don't go.*"

Already regretting her ill-considered outburst, Gloria said with a shrug: "Okay." She knew when she was licked. With a clever, pretty nurse on the premises, how could a worried, distraught wife hope to win?

She said no to Martha. She couldn't possibly eat a bite just now. Later, after she had Bobby settled for the night, she would go for a drive, get a sandwich and a malted while she was out.

An hour later Sue had Dave fixed in bed, his face sponged, his temperature read, the window at the far end of the room opened. With a dubious glance, she took the pills from the tiny plastic holder on the bedside table and put them where he could reach them easily if he had trouble sleeping. She *hoped* they were safe for him to take.

Shaking her head, as if to shake away all bothersome suspicions, she leaned over Dave. "Everything okay, honey?"

"Everything is wonderful," he murmured, reaching for her hand. "Thanks for everything, darling. For now and forever—thank you."

He closed his eyes, and still clutching her hand, fell asleep while she watched him.

Dimming the light, she left the room, closed the door softly behind her, and was on her way down the hall to her own room when she heard an angry scream from Gloria's room.

Bobby was shouting at the top of his lungs. "I want a key to my door. I ain't going to sleep 'less you give me a key."

Gloria's room, an enormous one, approximately thirty feet long, had an adjoining alcove the size of a small room. There was a window overlooking the side garden, a door, and a sofa bed which Gloria had made up for Bobby to sleep on.

As Sue walked in, asking what was wrong, Gloria seemed to have forgotten their recent unpleasantness. "Sue, sweetie, will you please help me talk sense to this boy?"

She supposed he was nervous because he was being put to bed in a strange room. Children were like that, weren't they? And Bobby was such a sensitive little boy, so high-strung and all.

Bobby, in his pajamas, had a wild look in his eyes. He stood beside the bed, scowling and definitely refusing to get into it.

"What seems to be the problem, pal?" Sue asked. "You afraid of ghosts or something?"

No, Bobby was not afraid of any old ghosts. In fact, he'd sort of like to meet a ghost if there was one around. "Man, I'd ask that ghost to sit right down."

Losing interest in this unlikely occurrence, he said flatly: "There's a key to that door, and I want it."

Upon further questioning, he said: "I want my door locked so nobody can sneak in and kill me while I'm asleep. That's why."

"Now, Bobby—" With an indulgent smile Sue told him: "You must know there's nobody in this house who would kill you. What put such an idea in your head?"

"A lot you know," muttered the boy.

Sue turned to ask Gloria: "There is a key to the door. Why not let him have it?"

"No." Gloria was firm. It was never wise to give in to a child's irrational demands. Give them an inch and they'd take a mile.

"I want that door open. I intend to have it open."

"I want the key so I can lock myself in." Bobby was screaming again, giving every sign of a first class tantrum, as Sue walked out, leaving mother and son to wrestle it out.

No doubt Gloria was right in her stand. But what was the boy scared of? That was absolute terror she had seen on his face. Why? What was the reason? Just a child's instinctive fear of the dark, the unknown?

Probably. But some vague hunch told her there was more to it than that.

Chapter 14

Marv sat in front of his fire, smoking, while he studied the report from the detective agency which had come to his office by Special Delivery late that afternoon. It was eight o'clock; he had finished the dinner of scrambled eggs, crisp bacon, and buttered toast which he had fixed for himself. He enjoyed cooking for himself and he preferred to eat alone, in the privacy of his cottage, especially when he had an urgent problem on his mind and was not at all sure how best to deal with it.

His current problem had two angles, each dovetailing into the other. Should he, or should he not, drive out to the Blue Dragon to meet Gloria? That was a minor problem—or was it?

When you were dealing with a truly dangerous individual (and here in his hands was the evidence that beautiful Gloria could be very dangerous), every little move should be given thoughtful consideration.

He mused, refilling his pipe, If I make an enemy of the gal, I might regret it.

It was not inconceivable that she might pose a deadly threat to everything and everyone he held dear.

He got up to poke at the fire, thinking how pleasant it would be to spend the evening there with a good book. To have a cat snuggling on his lap would be nice, too. Some day he must get a cat, preferably a Siamese.

Occasionally Marv admitted to himself that he was a lonely man. It would be nice to have a pretty, loving and beloved wife to come home to. But he had never wanted to take a chance on a girl who could be only second best. And for some men—for himself—maybe it just wasn't in the cards to have the one girl they had ever really wanted.

He sat down again. For a moment, although he had plenty else to think about, Marv allowed himself to dwell on thoughts of that girl. Why did the one unattainable woman seem so different from, so vastly more desirable than all the millions of others in the world?

Presently he sighed and turned his eyes and his attention back to the agency report, which gave the lie to Gloria's interesting story about the wealthy parents who had fought from court to court for her possession.

Gloria had never had any wealthy papa. The only time she had ever achieved newspaper mention was when, at age fourteen, she had battered a foster mother over the head with an iron skillet. Caught in the act of stealing around fifty dollars from its hiding place in the icebox, Gloria had taken to violence, and raced out of the house straight into the arms of a neighbor who had heard the old woman's screams.

It was the typical sordid story of a girl born in the New york slums; born of a father who ended up in the penitentiary, of a mother who refused to take any responsibility for a child she hadn't wanted to start with.

The kid had started out with the cards stacked against her, thought Marv. It would be easy to pity her—until he considered the woman she had tried to bludgeon to death for a few paltry dollars.

Following that almost deadly assault, the Welfare people had taken over. It was decided that Gloria had deep-seated emotional problems. What she needed was extensive psychiatric help. She was sent to an institution where disturbed children were analyzed, treated, every effort made to root out their basic problems, to reorient their relations to society and, hopefully, change them into useful, well adjusted members of that society.

A few days after her sixteenth birthday, Gloria was dismissed from the institution. She had, so her record stated, made an excellent readjustment.

She was on her own—a girl who had learned one very important fact from those brainy psychiatrists. She had learned that you could fool anybody if you set your mind to it and if you were clever. A lot the experts knew. She hadn't changed one iota. She had grown older, wiser, that was all. She still wanted money, the same as she had when she had gone after the woman's little horde in the icebox.

Of course, she was grown up now. And most important of all, she was a raving beauty.

Her looks were the big thing she had going for her, and some fine day her fabulous beauty would get her into the big chips.

Meanwhile, she was willing to work. . . .

Reading over the report, Marv had to fill in the more personal angles for himself, more or less dramatize the cut and dried facts set down by the investigator. But it was an easy matter to read between the lines, to sketch in for himself the character of this woman who had worked herself up from waitress to model to the fringes of show business in Hollywood, until now—

Again Marv glanced at his watch. Ten minutes to nine. "Meet me at the Blue Tavern at nine," she had said.

With the last, longing look at the fire, which was dying, Marv got up, went out to his car, and headed for the Blue Tavern.

I'll play it by ear, he decided as he drove down the highway. The main thing was to play for time. And if the worst came to the worst he would promise whatever the gal wanted him to promise. If necessary, just to allay her suspicions, he might have to pretend he thought her the loveliest, the most desirable woman in the world.

Being a vain woman, very much in love with herself, she would believe that.

He thought ruefully, swinging the car abruptly to avoid a careening car filled with shrieking teenagers, I feel as if I were going into battle. In a sense he was—a battle with a dangerous ruthless female who posed a threat to the brother he had always loved dearly, and to the girl he loved hopelessly.

He drove into the parking lot to the side of the Blue Tavern and nosed his car into an empty slot. Then he lit a cigarette and sat for some moments, thinking hard, engaged in a silent conversation with himself.

Isn't there the possibility that you're being unfair to Gloria? She wouldn't be the first gal or the last to try to cash in on the estate of a wealthy husband.

That's absolutely right.

She is a beautiful woman. You can't blame her for using her beauty for all it's worth.

Right again.

And as for trying to play tricks with you—well, be honest. Other women, even some of your clients, have resorted to all sorts of blandishments to get around you. There have been one or two who swore they couldn't live without you and quite possibly believed their own silly raving. Women are strange creatures. They seem able, some of them, to fall in love with the speed of light. So maybe Gloria truly imagines she's nuts about you.

Could be. Marv lit a second cigarette. He wished he was back by his fire with his pipe, a book, and that Siamese cat on his lap. Funny. Men usually preferred dogs. As for him, he'd take a cat, maybe because they were such fiercely independent little creatures. No man ever owned a cat. The cat owned the man.

So when you consider the matter objectively, is it fair to tag Gloria as actually a dangerous person? Is it sensible? Generally speaking, you are not an overly imaginative guy. But for once in your life, isn't it possible that you're allowing your imagination to run away with your better judgment?

This time, his face drawn in worried lines, Marv muttered his thoughts aloud.

"A girl who tried her hand at murder when she was fourteen? A girl who spent two years in a mental institution, under treatment as a potential psychotic?"

Why shouldn't he be scared of her?

She wouldn't be the first one to attempt murder and be set free to try it again.

Chapter 15

Sue woke up. She heard screaming. At first she thought she had been having a nightmare, that she had dreamed those shrill, hysterical sounds. But there it was again. She sat up, switched on the bed light, and looked at her watch. Ten past eleven. She had gone to bed a little after nine, so weary she'd been ready to fall asleep standing up.

The screaming came again. Wide awake now, she knew that it came from the far end of the hall, from Gloria's room. Bobby? Now she made out the frantic words: *"Let me out!"*

She leaped out of bed, wrapping on her robe as she raced, barefooted, down the hall into Gloria's room, where a light burned dimly.

But there was no Gloria, no sign of her. The bed had not been slept in; the blue gown at the foot of it had not been worn. "Let me out, let me out!"

Now the words were accompanied by the pounding of frenzied fists on the door which led into Bobby's sleeping alcove.

The words died away, lost in a child's hopeless sobbing as Sue crossed the room and put her ear to the door.

"What's wrong, honey?"

"I can't get out. I got up 'cause I had to go to the bathroom. And she's got me locked in. Oh, let me out. Please, please let me out."

"Maybe you've locked yourself in, Bobby." That seemed the logical explanation. Gloria must have had a change of heart, decided to let the boy have the key. Then he had gone to sleep and forgotten about it.

"The key must be in the door, darling. All you have to do is give it a turn."

But she was wrong about that, and after a few more minutes of Bobby's frantic sobbing, after he had said over and over that there wasn't any key—not in the lock, or on the floor, or anywhere—what must have happened began to come clear.

"What's going on, for goodness' sakes?" Martha spoke from the doorway, then came hurrying in. "That boy sounds as if he's having a fit of some sort."

"He's scared," Sue said, and began to search the floor on her side of the door. "Is there a spare key, Martha?"

"No," said Martha, explaining that there had been a second key but it had been lost. "Where is Gloria?" Why wasn't that woman there to look after her child? It was almost midnight. *Where was she?*

"I have no idea." Right then the sobbing on the far side of the door gave way to the retching sounds of a child being very, very sick.

Having searched everywhere they could think of—on the dressing table, under Gloria's pillow, even under the bed—Sue and Martha stood staring at each other.

"I suppose we could call the fire department," Martha said. "They could bring a ladder, climb up to the window and get in."

Sue shook her head, the nurse in her alert to what that would mean to Dave. No matter how deep in sleep he might be, thanks to the pills which might or might not be doped, the sound of a fire truck, men climbing around outside the house, would jar him awake.

"If you don't let me out, I'm gonna jump out the window!" Bobby had revived and was screaming again.

"Where do you suppose that woman has gone to, Sue?"

But it was perfectly clear that Gloria had gone somewhere, that it had been her purpose right along to sneak out of the house. That, thought Sue, was the reason she had refused to let Bobby have a key. She had her own plans, whatever they were. As soon as the coast was clear, she had locked Bobby in his room so that he couldn't go wandering around the house creating a disturbance, giving away the fact that she was gone.

Martha had gone back to the door and was trying to calm the hysterical child. "We'll get you out of there as soon as we can, honey. Don't be frightened. I'll stay right here, only a few inches away. Sue is going to hunt for your mother. She'll be here with the key before you know it."

"I hate her! She locked me in on purpose. I guess maybe she thought the house would catch on fire and I'd get burned to death."

"Now, sweetheart, don't say things like that. Your mother loves you."

"That old Gloria don't love me. She—"

"Well, I love you. Sue loves you. Your daddy loves you."

"He's my big brother, like they say on TV. They say every little boy needs a big brother. So when I asked him, would he be my big brother, he said he would."

"All right, darling. Your big brother loves you. Now will you try to be a little patient while Sue goes to look for your mother?"

Bobby's reply was a faint whimper.

"Maybe she's gone to the Blue Tavern," Sue said, suddenly recalling something Myrtle, the little maid, had let slip.

"I wouldn't put it past her." Martha's tone implied that only a thoroughly depraved woman would go to such a notorious cocktail bar, especially without an escort.

Sue didn't even bother to dress. There wasn't time. She had had enough experience with troubled children to understand that Bobby was undergoing a traumatic experience which could create a lasting personality problem.

Rushing to her room, she pulled on a cashmere coat over her robe, rushed out to her car, then turned back, wondering if Marv was in his cottage. Why hadn't she thought of him sooner? He was the logical one to call on for help.

The cottage was dark. No amount of pounding on the door brought any results. Out on a date, Sue assumed, and rushed back to the garage, into her car, and for the first time in her life found herself pushing the speedometer to ninety miles an hour. Down the highway she raced.

The Blue Tavern was a typical posh night spot, with dim lights, a long semicircular bar and booths to one side.

"Just a minute, miss." A female wearing a reddish wig that looked rather like a hornet's nest tried to bar her way.

Sue brushed her aside. "I'm looking for someone," Sue said. "It's an emergency, I'm a nurse. Is that clear?"

Her glance scanned the faces at the bar as she made her way through the semi-darkness. There were a number of blondes, but no sign of Gloria.

Then she turned her attention to the booths. . . .

She heard Gloria's laugh before she actually located the table where the laugh came from. Someone must have once told Gloria that her laugh was like the tinkle of bells, because at times, especially after a few too many martinis, it was so obviously intended to tinkle that it jangled.

Then came Gloria's voice, loud and clear. "I

mean every word I'm saying, Marv darling. Once everything is settled, I want you to take me to Paris. We'll have all that money to spend, and I've always longed to see Paris in the spring with the man I love. Won't we have fun?"

Tinkle, tinkle.

Sue walked straight to the table. Her eyes flashed daggers at Marv before she glanced at his companion.

How fabulous Gloria looked: a vision of blonde beauty swathed in black; glitter from crysal eardrops, from bracelets and necklace.

She'd be stunning riding a white horse at a circus, Sue thought, and said: "I'm sorry to crash in on love's pretty dream, Gloria. But Bobby is threatening to jump out the window and kill himself. Would you please give me the key to his door?"

"Oh, that impossible brat!" Obviously this ill-considered remark was the last martini talking, as was the one that followed.

"Don't worry about him, Sue. The kid is just putting on an act." Again the tinkle, tinkle, which now came out a decided giggle. "Bobby is a marvelous little actor."

Later Sue was to recall that remark. At the moment she paid no attention to it.

Gloria had straightened up and suddenly snapped: "I see through you. You're in love with Marv, and you're jealous. You followed us here; then you thought up this silly lie about Bobby.

You're out to make trouble, aren't you? You're trying to turn Marv against me. Oh, I see through you. But it won't work, Nurse. This guy is all mine. Now get out of here. Let us alone."

With that she tossed the remains of her drink into Sue's face and began to laugh raucously. Marv got up, pulled her to her feet, and said quietly: "Come along, Gloria. Let's get out of here. I want to know what this is all about. Did you lock the boy in?"

"I told you," Gloria said when they were outside. She was still laughing. "The kid is putting on an act."

They walked to Marv's car, since Gloria was in no condition to drive. She was glaring at Sue. "You're after my man, and you're to let him alone. I'm warning you. Understand?" Then she slapped Sue in the face.

"I don't know anything about the darned key," Gloria muttered as Marv lifted her bodily into the car. "If she don't keep away from my man, I'll kill her." Marv had the wisdom not to argue with her. After a few more dark threats, she passed out.

His face drawn in grave, worried lines, Marv walked Sue to the slot where her car was parked. "I'm so very sorry," he began, and was interrupted by Sue's curt retort.

"This is scarcely the time for meaningless talk. All I want is the key. It's up to you to get it from her before that boy goes into serious convulsions from terror."

"She claims she doesn't have it, Sue."

She said not a word, but the look she gave him said clearly: "I suppose the key locked the door by itself, twisted out of the keyhole, and walked away."

"I'll see you at the house," Marv called as Sue slid in behind the wheel and drove away.

Chapter 16

It was four o'clock when Sue finally got back to bed. The key had been tucked away in Gloria's purse. After unlocking the door, Marv still had the worried look of a proud and decent man caught in an embarrassing and distasteful situation certainly not to his liking. But he said very little as he helped with the boy.

Marv had a nice way with children. Bobby seemed to take to him, trust him, on sight. When Sue finally left the room, after she and Martha had straightened and cleaned things, Marv was still sitting on the bed, Bobby's damp little hand clutching his. "I'll sleep here right beside you, kid," he was promising.

Gloria was in one of the spare bedrooms, dead to the world.

Once she was alone in her room, Sue sank down on the bed, slumped forward, her face buried in her hands. Her body trembled with the sobs which she tried to explain away as nervous and physical exhaustion.

But she was lying to herself. Her weary feet, her aching muscles, tension from worry and nerves strung tight, had little to do with the tears that streamed down her flushed cheeks. She sat weeping for a long while. When she finally got up to throw off her robe, she looked in the mirror. Her eyes were red and swollen; she looked awful.

It was all over. Telling herself over and over that her feeling for Marv was nothing more than an adolescent hangup, that she must kill it once and for all, had not worked. The tiny shred of hope had lived on. It had refused to die. He loved her. Somehow, sooner or later, the miracle would happen. All self-delusion. A lie she had clung to while she went on with her foolish dreaming.

Now she knew the truth. He was in love with Gloria, or if not actually in love, so wildly and helplessly infatuated that he would do whatever she asked him to do. Nothing else could explain their rendezvous at the Blue Tavern. No doubt there had been other such dates, and there was no explanation except that Gloria had him wound around her finger.

Essentially Marv was a man of character, with standards of honesty and loyalty. It was not in character for him to sneak out to a notorious night spot with his brother's wife while Dave lay ill, possibly dying. Yet he had done that. *Paris in the spring. What fun we'll have!*

There they had sat, Gloria making her plans, deciding what they would do with Dave's money when Dave was gone. All this Sue had heard. But had she heard Marv utter one word of objection, or disapproval? Had he so much as raised his voice to say it was not right or decent to discuss such plans at this time?

No.

Oh, she's got him hooked, Sue thought bleakly. And what kind of an idiot was she to be shedding one single tear over losing him? *Losing him?* How silly could she get? she wondered, and rushed to the bathroom to splash water over her burning tear-streaked face.

How could a girl lose a man who had never been hers except in her dreams?

Back in the room, she stood taking several deep breaths and swore to herself that she would never waste another thought on Marv Crowell. Then, abruptly, the tears started again.

Throwing herself over the bed, her body again shuddered with sobs. How could he? *How could he?*

She thought that she could never stop crying and go to sleep—but when she woke up Martha was standing beside the bed with a breakfast tray, a cheery smile and the news that she had another patient.

"Patient? Who?"

"Bobby." The boy had developed an angry rash. It looked like measles.

Martha's smile widened as if her further item of news filled her with delight. "Gloria has developed a fine attack of hysterics."

"You mean a hangover?" Sue sat up, sipping

coffee with pleasure. Nobody could make coffee as good and strong as Martha could.

No hangover, asserted the old lady. Indeed no. When Gloria got up, went into Bobby's room and saw the unsightly rash on the boy's face and neck—"Well, you should have heard her as she came screaming downstairs, telling me to get the boy as far away from her room as possible. It sounded as if she expected me to put him out in the garage, maybe, carrying on like she was out of her mind."

Chuckling, Martha seated herself on the edge of the bed. "Guess she was afraid she'd catch the disease and break out in spots; afraid it would ruin her fatal beauty."

And so, Martha went on, they must plan what to do. Moving Bobby into the small room adjoining Sue's bedroom seemed the best idea. "When you're busy with Bobby, I can look after Dave."

Not, she went on sadly, that there was much to be done for her beloved boy. Sooner or later his life would just flicker out, like a candle flame. Wiping a quick tear from her eye, she said softly: "I'm trying to learn to accept it."

Dr. Ronald Brown came later that day. After taking the boy's temperature, pondering over the cough, the runny nose, as well as the rash, he pronounced: "Yes, measles."

Which made it official.

Sue kept her doubts to herself. Measles developed from a virus infection. What was more, there were certain signs which accompanied the onslaught of measles; primarily Koplik spots just opposite the lower grinding molars. Dr. Brown had not bothered to look for such spots. It was conceivable, thought Sue, that he had never heard of Koplik spots.

But Sue had looked. There were no spots.

It was Sue's firm conviction that the rash, as well as Bobby's feverish condition, were psychomatic. His terror last night had put too much of a strain on his young, tortured mind. The unsightly physical rash was the result.

But the all-wise Dr. Brown said it was measles. He went on to warn Gloria that she must be very, very careful, because the infection could easily be transmitted, person to person.

This sent lovely, glamorous Gloria into a second attack of near hysterics. "I knew it," she cried, adding that it would be too horrible if she were to catch it. "Oh, move the boy somewhere, anywhere." And wasn't there some spray she could use to disinfect the room where he had slept?

"I'd absolutely die if I got the measles!"

Dr. Brown patted her shoulder comfortingly, assured her that with the proper precautions there was nothing to worry about, and went on his way.

"It couldn't have worked out better," said Martha later, in the kitchen. Now she and Sue between them could look after the poor boy properly, give him the love and understanding he sadly needed.

Martha never spoke of Bobby as her grandchild,

but obviously she had taken a warm liking to him. "Poor little bairn," she said. He didn't know what it was like to have a taste of true mother love. You only had to take one look at Gloria, and anybody with a grain of sense could tell she didn't have a spark of honest, maternal affection in her.

During the rest of that day and the next, Bobby seemed content to lie quietly, sleeping much of the time. "I ain't hungry," he would say when Sue brought in a cup of broth or a glass of orange juice.

"I'm so awful, awful tired."

Well, who wouldn't be tired? Who wouldn't look wan; for that matter, who wouldn't break out in a rash, after the terrified hours the boy had been forced to endure?

Sue tried to imagine what it would be like to be six years old (although Bobby certainly looked closer to eight, but never mind that) and to find herself locked up in a strange room, in a strange house, with no one to come and unlock the door, set you free, no matter how much you screamed and pummeled the wall.

She couldn't imagine it.

I'd break out in a rash, too, Sue thought that evening when she went into Dave's room and tried to explain why Bobby had been put to bed and was being kept more or less in isolation.

Measles. With Dave, it seemed best to go along with Dr. Brown's diagnosis. To tell him what had actually happened wouldn't be wise.

The trouble was, Dave wasn't buying her story.

Not that he said it in so many words. But he gave her a slow, wavering smile and reached for her hand as he told her: "I'm worried about the kid, Sue. Basically, he's a fine boy. I've taken a real liking to him. But—"

He sighed, obediently sipping water from the glass Sue held to his unsteady lips. "The way I've got him figured out, Bobby is starved for love. He desperately needs a friend he can trust. After I'm gone, be a friend to him, honey. *Don't desert Bobby.*"

She did not know what to say. Remind Dave that Bobby would have his mother?

She even considered asking him if he had decided to make the financial provision for the boy that Gloria was so desperately determined to have him make.

But she had better not. This had been one of the days when Dave gave every evidence that he was losing the battle against time and his illness.

He had spent most of the day in bed, saying that he lacked the strength, even the desire, to make the effort to get up. His appetite had vanished. His eyes looked sick.

It was no time to remind him that time was running out by mentioning his will.

To her surprise, Dave himself brought up the subject. Maybe he had been reading her mind.

He said: "Marv tells me I should make a new will, and he's right. There's quite a bit of money involved. I wouldn't want to die with it on my conscience that I had done anyone an injustice."

Sue walked away from the bed, pretending to rearrange the roses in the white pottery bowl on the table in front of one window. She did not want Dave to see her eyes. They must reflect the sense of outrage which for a moment seemed to consume her.

"Marv tells me I should make a new will."

So that he and Gloria could have fun in Paris in the spring?

He and Marv had talked it all over very carefully, Dave was saying. They were in perfect agreement as to how his estate should be disposed of, who should get what, and under what conditions. "I've given Marv a free hand," he said, "in the writing of the will."

Sue drew several deep breaths. She longed to tell him: "You poor fool, you blessed, trusting idiot. Can't you understand that you're being had by two designing people? A man who pretends to be your loving brother, a woman who pretends to be your loving wife?"

She didn't say it.

All she said was, "Okay," when he told her, even if he was asleep, she was to tell Marv to come up to his room whenever he came with the will to be signed.

Marv had been closeted with Dave for an hour that same afternoon. That, she guessed, was when it had all been settled. Hurrah for Marv! You had to give him credit. He hadn't let any grass grow under his feet after last night.

She went back to Bobby's room, resolving as she went to ignore Marv Crowell's existence from then on.

Unhappily, that was difficult to do. He was in and out of Bobby's room a dozen times during the next two days.

Giving the excuse that he felt he was needed here, what with all the sickness and confusion, Marv explained that he was taking a few days off from the office. No, he wasn't afraid of Bobby's germs, or whatever. Heck, he had had measles when he was a kid. Once you'd had the disease, you'd had it.

"And I don't have to worry about a few spots marring my ugly mug," he told Gloria, when she warned him that he was taking a terrible risk.

Gloria herself did not enter the room during those first days. Apparently she felt uneasy about the house itself. She would go out in her car, absent herself for hours.

When she returned, neither Sue nor Martha would ask where she had been; not because they hesitated to pry, but because they couldn't have cared less. When Gloria left the house it was as if an unpleasant cloud had lifted. The longer she stayed away, the better.

"Vacation is over," Marv announced. That was on the morning of the fourth day after Bobby was taken ill. "See you tonight, fellow," he promised the boy who had decided that his friend, Marv, was the greatest guy in the world.

"You promise you'll be back tonight?"

"I promise."

"Will you bring me a present?"

"Sure. How about an ice cream cone?"

"Nope. I'm sick of ice cream cones."

"Okay, buddy. You name it. Want a puppy?"

The boy's eyes shone.

"Or how about a kitten?" A kitten, Marv pointed out, was easier to take care of than a dog. Kittens, for some reason, were born knowing how to take care of themselves. They could talk to a fellow, too.

"Aw, you're fooling me. Cats can't talk."

"Sure they can. Siamese cats talk their heads off. They're as bad as gabby women."

Bobby giggled. He didn't know what to believe. Still, his new-found friend, Marv, never lied to him.

"Okay," he said finally, taking a deep breath. "You bring me a kitten that can talk." At which point Sue was forced to address Marv directly for the first time in two days. "Now listen," she began.

There was no point in making a promise he couldn't keep. Bring a kitten into the house at a time like this, when she and Martha had their hands full! "Who would look after it?"

Dear, sweet Gloria? She had not meant to let venom creep into her voice, but after all, she was only human.

Marv laughed heartily. Frankly, it was hard for him to picture Gloria cuddling a little kitten in her arms. Cats were a lot like humans. They needed lots of love and affection.

"You seem to know quite a lot about cats," Sue retorted coldly, thinking it a pity he didn't know more about the human variety of cats.

Yes, Marv grinned, he did indeed. He had made quite a study of cats. For instance, did Sue happen to know that the cat was once considered a sacred animal and treated as such? "Why, you take the ancient Egyptians—"

"I neither know," said Sue, "nor care." Not that she had anything against cats. In fact, she *liked* cats. But this was neither the time nor the place—

"Fine," Marv approved. "That makes a very real bond between us. With a mutual love of felines going for us, I'd say we belong together. What would you say?"

"I'd say I'm fed up with this nonsensicial talk." Sue had taken Bobby's temperature, which was down close to normal. The rash was still evident, but otherwise he seemed a lot better. He was livelier, getting restless. She crossed the room to open a window. "And it's very wrong to make a promise to a child that you know you can't keep."

"I want a kitten to love and cuddle," Bobby cried.

"And you're going to have it," Marv said quite seriously. Then with equal seriousness he told Sue: "I'll keep it over at my place until Bobby is back on his feet." Later Bobby could take on the responsibility of looking after it.

Sue was confused. All that morning she wondered about Marv's unexpected interest in Bobby. It bothered her because it did not fit in with the character of the infatuated man who was engaging in a surreptitious and, to her way of thinking, unscrupulous romance with Gloria. Only men who had never really grown up lost their common sense, even their sense of right and wrong, simply because a woman was beautiful and entrancing.

Yet when it comes to Bobby, honestly, ran Sue's confused thoughts, he's as concerned as if he were the boy's wise father.

Of course! Maybe that was the answer! He was in training to be Bobby's dad because he counted on being exactly that. The answer was so simple it was laughable.

It was also a reminder to put Marv out of her mind and keep him out. Lordy, how long was it going to take her to learn that simple lesson?

As soon as he had eaten his lunch that day, Bobby announced that he wanted to get up. He thought maybe he'd like to dress and go down to the ocean for a swim. Or maybe he'd settle for a movie. He loved movies. No, TV wouldn't do. He was sick of television. He wanted to go out.

Sue tried to reason with him, drawing a chair up beside the bed. "Now listen, honey." He could not be allowed out of bed until the rash was more or less gone, nor until his temperature came down and stayed down.

"You don't want to get real sick all over again, do you?"

"I want to get out of this old bed."

"You must be a little patient, sweetie."

Bobby scowled, he muttered to himself, he refused to play any games, he didn't want Sue or Martha to read him any silly old stories. "I'm going nuts," said Bobby.

And so am I, thought Sue. She should lecture the child about patience! By mid-afternoon her own patience had just about run out. Bobby was being as brattish as a restless, highly energized, strong-willed six-year-old could possibly be.

"I want to do something different," Bobby cried, and began to sob. He was sick of being shut up and stuck in the old bed and being treated like a little old baby.

It was when he began to kick at the covers, to scream and threaten to sneak out and run away when nobody was looking, that Sue asked: "Would you like me to tell your fortune, honey?"

The idea was born of sheer desperation. Anything to quiet him down. As Sue explained later to Martha: "I was afraid he was going into convulsions."

"What's my fortune?" A bright and curious boy, Bobby's attention invariably was caught by something he did not understand.

Sue tried to explain as best she could.

First of all, it was strictly a fun thing. From the beginning of time, she said, there had been certain individuals who pretended they could tell another person all about his past and what was going to happen in the future. Sometimes they would look into a crystal ball and pretend they saw pictures in it. It was all make-believe, but—

"What kind of pictures?" Bobby interrupted.

Well, sometimes pictures of people—a boy's mother or father or his friends. Then, still pretending, they would make up a story about what was going to happen to these people, or had happened.

"Have you got a crystal ball?" demanded Bobby, his young face twisted in furious thought.

Because if she had—"I want to look in it. I'll bet I can see my mummy in it. Maybe my dad, too."

Curious. It was the first time she had heard Bobby refer to Gloria as his mummy. She wondered why he said it now, and told him: "I just may have one stuck away in my bag, honey. I'll go see."

Chapter 17

"You must remember," Sue repeated before she put the ball into Bobby's impatient hands, "this is just a fun thing. Understand?"

"Yeah."

"I don't expect you to see a thing in it, sweetie. And if you do, it's only your imagination. Do you understand what imagination means?"

"Yeah. It's when you're kidding yourself."

Sue smiled. "Now this crystal ball is actually just a piece of quartz which is transparent. Sometimes it is described as smoly quartz."

"Gimme," said Bobby, trying to snatch the ball, which already seemed to fascinate him. "Stop teasing me with all them funny words."

"I am not teasing you, sweetheart." All she wanted, she explained earnestly, was to have him understand that he must not take the ball seriously. Clearly it would be impossible for him to see pictures or people in what was simply a piece of mineral.

"Aw, stop yakking about it," Bobby muttered.

"That isn't very polite, honey."

"I got the measles. I've been a very ill boy with a

fever. And I'm all messed up with germs. So I don't have to be polite."

Then, with one of his rare smiles and a complete change of approach: "May I have the crystal ball, please?"

Laughing, Sue put the ball in his hot little hands and went downstairs to tell Martha she didn't know whether she had done the right thing or not.

"You don't suppose the child will get any wild ideas, do you?" Children were so impressionable. And Bobby was such a confused, mixed up boy in some ways. "It would be just like him," she went on worriedly, "to start imagining he did see things in that piece of glass."

"You worry too much," said Martha placidly. She was at the sink scraping what she estimated to be her thousandth carrot in the past week. If Edith Garber, her housekeeper, didn't soon recover from the flu and return to work, the number would probably run into the billions. Martha was a firm believer in the food value of raw carrots.

"And what if he does see things you don't believe are there to be seen?" It was a well known fact that many children were psychic. When they reported seeing things that older people considered nonsense, it did not necessarily mean that they were lying or would grow up to be lunatics.

Sue's smile was amused as she went to the icebox, wondering if Dave could eat a broiled lamb chop for dinner.

"Now Martha, don't tell me you put any stock in

crystal gazing and all that nonsense."

Martha tossed her pretty white head, held the scraper under the hot spigot, and asserted that she didn't call something nonsense just because she did not understand it.

"But I'll tell you this much." And she related the story about the time she had had her fortune told. A woman, as nice and sincere a woman as you'd ever meet, had stared into a crystal ball. "The things she told me were absolutely weird." It had been twenty years ago, and some of her prophecies were still coming true.

"Among other things—" Martha began, just as Bobby's voice, all excited, called for Sue to come upstairs quickly.

"Are you feeling sick, honey?" Worried, Sue hurried up to his room, Martha right behind her.

"I saw her!" His childish voice quivered with excitement; dark eyes were aglow. "I saw my mummy in the crystal ball. She had golden hair and she was dressed in white, and she looked like an angel. And she was holding out her arms to me. And she said she loved me and was watching over me from up in heaven."

"I could kick myself for letting him have that ball," Sue said. She sat in Martha's room watching Martha, who was putting on a fresh dress for dinner. "I might have known he would start making things up."

"I wonder why he made up a story about his mother." Martha looked extremely thoughtful.

"That's easy to explain."

"All right, dear. You explain it." Martha smiled sweetly, and continued to smile while Sue told her how many children made up dream parents because they weren't satisfied with the ones they had. It was a kind of phase lots of children went through. They imagined they were adopted, for instance. In Bobby's case—well, obviously Gloria had been anything but the ideal mother. And until the last week or so, he had never been told a thing about his father. The poor child probably felt lost, as if he didn't belong to anybody. So—he had just dreamed up this beautiful mother who was in heaven and still loved him dearly.

It was that simple.

"You do make it sound very simple," Martha agreed, asking Sue to fasten an irritating zipper which invariably got stuck.

"But let's wait and see what else Bobby sees, or thinks he sees, in his ball. Shall we?"

"Martha!" Sue stared, shocked. "Don't tell me you believe that boy actually *saw* what he claims he saw."

Martha said calmly: "What I believe is that there's more to his story than meets the eye. We haven't enough sense to understand what it is."

Sue frowned. "I don't think we should encourage these wild tales," she said, just as the extension phone rang.

"That was Gloria," Martha said, her voice tart as it always was when she referred to her daughter-in-law. She cradled the receiver. "It seems she's dining with an old friend and won't be home until later."

Instantly Sue wondered if the "old friend" was Marv, and was still wondering about it when she went back to Bobby's room.

There was Marv. He was standing by the bed with a grin, in his arms a Siamese cat that was meowing like mad.

"His name is Mr. Kim," said Marv to the boy, who was standing up in the bed, shouting with delight.

"Is he mine? Is he really and truly mine?"

The next several minutes were hectic. Once he had the cat in his arms, Bobby settled back against the pillows, his young face radiant. It was the first time Sue had seen the youngster look truly happy.

That made it seem absolutely cruel to say the cat could not stay in the room. But what else could she do?

"I don't want to be unreasonable, Marv. But you surely must know things have to be sanitary in a sick room."

Marv looked puzzled. "I haven't the wildest idea what you're talking about, honey."

"Don't call me honey!"

"Okay, Nurse. I just don't understand why you consider a cat unsanitary. As a matter of fact, cats are cleaner than people. A cat will spend a good part of his time washing himself. If you've ever observed—"

"Oh, stop that idiotic talk." He was baiting her; that was what made her so furious. And when she was furious, how could she have the dignity and calm of an efficient, well trained nurse who was in complete control of the situation?

"Cats have fleas," she informed him. "Their hairs fly all over the place." Not, she conceded, that this wasn't a very beautiful cat. But it did not belong on Bobby's bed.

"Now take it out of here. That's an order."

"Mr. Kim is mine, and I want him." Bobby was screaming and scowling. "I want him right here in bed with me."

"Now see what you've started," Sue snorted, while Mr. Kim made a flying leap to the foot of the bed, muttered to himself, settled down and proceeded to wash his face.

Bobby was still yelling and threatening dire action if he couldn't have his cat.

Marv suddenly looked penitent, or pretended to. "I'm sorry if I'm upsetting sickroom procedure, Sue. My intentions were good. I wanted to please the kid, and I thought a pet would be company for him. I guess I just didn't think."

Sue gave him a frosty stare.

Then, since she couldn't make up her mind what to do, she went downstairs and set about preparing Dave's dinner. Martha seemed amused when she heard about the cat.

"Marv was always a great one for cats," she said, as if that were the point at issue. And when Sue mentioned the inadvisability of having an animal in a sick room, Martha chuckled.

Then she astonished Sue by telling her: "I don't believe it's the cat that's bothering you, child. I think you're just plain mad at Marv. You don't want to tell him right out that you don't like his carrying on with Gloria. So you're picking a fuss over a nice little cat."

Sue was silent for a moment, considering Martha's words. Then she said, wanting to be honest: "Possibly you're right." But this was no time to talk out her feelings, her disillusionment and her hurts. Martha was her good, dear friend; no doubt she would understand if Sue confided in her. It might be a relief to do just that.

But meanwhile, Dave's soup would get cold, and his chops would burn to a crisp.

"And stop worrying so much over Bobby," advised Martha as Sue started out of the kitchen, carrying Dave's tray.

"You know as well as I do, there's nothing seriously wrong with the child. Let him have his crystal ball and his cat. Let him have a little happiness."

It was after eight o'clock when Sue went into Bobby's room to get him ready for the night. She found him on the floor playing with Mr. Kim, who found the crystal ball to his liking. Bobby would give the ball a push, and cat would go scampering after it.

Sue laughed. It really was an adorable cat.

"Bobby—" She made him sit on the bed and look at her. "I love you very much," she told him. "I don't want to deny you anything that will give you pleasure, as long as it won't do you any harm."

But, on the other hand, she must be the one to decide what was best for him. "I cannot allow the kitty to sleep in here with you tonight. You're still a sick boy, and it wouldn't be good for you."

"Okay." The boy scowled, not at all pleased. But he was willing to give in about the cat, if she promised to take it straight over to his friend Marv, so nothing would happen to it.

But when Sue wanted to take the crystal ball, to put it away in a safe place, Bobby geared himself for a fight to the end. His face worked, his body stiffened.

"I've just got to keep it right here where I can touch it, maybe see things in it if I wake up in the night."

"Stop making things up, honey. You don't see pictures in that piece of glass. You mustn't tell fibs."

"I am not fibbing." He said it as earnestly as if he were telling the absolute truth.

Just a little while ago, insisted the boy, he had seen his daddy in the ball. "I saw him as plain as anything."

"You mean you saw Daddy Dave?"

"No." An emphatic shake of his head. Dave was his big brother. The man he had seen was his *real* daddy. "He was big and he smiled at me. He had on a uniform with lots of medals." A deep, deep sigh. "My real daddy was a hero."

For a moment Sue studied the boy's face thoughtfully. There was more to his story than met the eye, Martha had argued. Could she possibly be right?

Abruptly Bobby climbed out of the bed. "Come here, Kitty," he coaxed, explaining that he wanted Mr. Kim to have one more game before Sue took him away for the night.

"Come on, Kitty." The boy spun the crystal ball on the floor. The cat considered the situation, chattered briefly to himself, then made a graceful flying leap, his paw giving the ball a push which moved it a few inches.

While Mr. Kim gave thought to his next move, Gloria's voice shrilled from the doorway. "Where did that thing come from?"

"You mean the cat?" Sue turned. "Marv brought it to Bobby."

"I'm talking about that glass ball."

Sue stared at Gloria's contorted face.

"Who brought that ball in here?"

"It's mine," Sue said. "I gave it to Bobby to play with. For goodness sakes, Gloria, it's only a toy."

"A toy!" Gloria snapped tensely. Then with gritted teeth, she moved slowly toward Bobby. It was the first time since the rash appeared that she had come near him. "Give me that *thing*," she snapped.

"No."

"Did you hear what I said? You wretched

child!" Gone was all pretense of being a loving, doting mother. Gone, too, apparently, was her fear of the rash as her hand shot out, giving him a stinging blow over the cheek.

"It's mine and you can't have it."

"We'll see about that." Bending down to grab the ball from Mr. Kim, who had moved into a defensive position, covering it with his paw, Gloria moved quickly.

But Bobby was quicker.

His furious little hand pushed the ball to safety under the bed. Promptly the cat went scampering after it, and after the cat went Bobby. He emerged on the far side of the bed, wedged in against the wall. Ball in hand, his face was the embodiment of scowling, defiant determination.

"You try to take it, and you'll wish you hadn't." There was a curious tone in the boy's voice that sent a wave of foreboding through Sue's mind. "There's something we don't understand," Martha had said.

Gloria evidently had given up the battle. But she was breathing hard, and there was an awful expression in her eyes. She did not look altogether sane.

Better try to pacify her, Sue decided, and said: "Look, why make a big production out of such a small matter? I happened to have the crystal ball stuck in my bag. A nurse friend gave it to me. She used to tell fortunes with it. She believed in such nonsense, but I don't. I'm sure you don't either. I gave it to Bobby to play with because he was restless, and it seemed to amuse him."

She broke off. She felt as if she were talking to empty air. Gloria gave no sign that she had heard a word. On her face was the staring, distorted look of someone suddenly possessed of another personality.

"She was lying," Gloria muttered. "She had to be lying."

"Who was lying?" Sue asked.

Gloria's reply was laughter, high and shrill, as she walked out of the room and down the hall.

Shuddering, Sue wondered if it could possibly be that Gloria was losing her mind.

Chapter 18

Death came to Dave Harding during the night, exactly one week later. It was a shock, as the passing of someone loved and close is always a shock. "You tell yourself you'll be brave, ready to let them go," Martha said. "But when the time comes, you never are ready."

Sue was shocked, and not only because Dave was so closely linked with her youth, with her first dream of romantic love. There was that, of course, and in a sense it was if when Dave went, he took her youth with him, as if a part of herself had died.

But there was something else that bothered her. *Why* had it happened on this particular night, exactly two nights after Marv had come with the new will and his office secretary to witness the signing? Sue herself had been the second signatory.

The strange thing was that for some days Dave had given every evidence that he was picking up strength. And then he was gone. He simply fell asleep, after taking the pills which Gloria made a nightly rite of putting into the tiny plastic box —and he did not wake up.

After the funeral services, on a Thursday, Marv

asked everyone to come into the library, a small room which faced the side garden. He wanted Bobby present, too, while he read Dave's will.

Bobby came, insisting on bringing his two boon companions: Mr. Kim in his arms, the crystal ball bulging in the pocket of his cardigan. The rash had pretty well cleared up, and Bobby looked his customary scowling, determined young self.

"You sit there near the door, kid," Marv directed. That way, if the cat wanted out, as cats were wont to do, the door would be handy.

Martha sat in an easy chair beside the open fire, where a log was burning lazily. Sue, sitting beside her, covered Martha's hand with her own.

If only I could give her some real comfort, Sue thought, watching the older woman trying to fight back the tears which kept filling her eyes.

Gloria sat in lonely splendor on the far side of the room. She was dressed in black, as befitted a grieving widow. But as she sat with legs crossed, the black sheath slipped up above her knees, revealing the sheerest nylon encasing shapely legs, beautiful ankles, and high arched feet slipped into jeweled sandals. Her hair was a shimmering shawl of pale gold reaching to her shoulders. Her earrings were enormous loops of imitation diamonds which sparkled, as did the necklace roped around her slender throat. She looked fabulous.

She wore a smile, too, a smile which reminded Sue of a cat which had just caught a canary.

Maybe I'm just plain jealous, admitted Sue ruefully to herself. She can't help being so beautiful. Marv can't help being crazy about her because she is beautiful. And I can't help disliking her for the same reason.

I should, thought Sue, be darned well ashamed of myself. Why don't I grow up?

Marv, from his chair beside a small end table, was reading the will. There were a number of small bequests, and a generous provision for Martha, his mother, for her lifetime.

Next came a list of various charities to which he left generous amounts.

At which point Gloria spoke up, irritated. "All that money to charity! Poor Dave's mind must have been slipping."

Sue's glance flickered to Martha, who was saying gently: "It was his money, Gloria. And Dave always believed in helping those less fortunate than himself."

"Oh, I know." Gloria took a deep breath, and the earrings swung and glittered. "But the way I look at it, charity should begin at home."

Marv cleared his throat. "I'd like to finish this without further interruptions, Gloria, if you don't mind."

"Oh, read on." She uncrossed, then recrossed her legs. "But it is rather—well, I wonder if poor Dave knew what he was doing."

Marv glanced at her, his smile faint. "Oh, I

assure you, my dear, he knew exactly what he was doing." He cleared his throat again.

"And we now come to the part that directly concerns you."

It was a few moments before Sue clearly grasped the trend of what Marv was reading, and not because of the legal verbiage. On the contrary, it did not sound legal at all.

A long, extensive paragraph was devoted to a review of his marriage to Gloria, her desertion of him, and made it altogether clear that she had no legal claim on his estate, because she had refused to live with him as his wife.

However, if, as she now claimed, there had been a son born of that brief marriage, well and good. He would overlook the past. He would accord her the rights of a wife who had continued to live with him during the past seven years. He would leave to her the remainder of his estate, of whatever nature, trusting her to do the right thing by their son.

With this in mind, he directed his half-brother, Marvin Crowell, named as the executor of his estate, to employ a detective agency to make a thorough investigation of said Bobby's birth et cetera. This must include signed statements by the doctor and nurse who were present at the boy's birth. It should also include an examination of the boy's birth certificate, so as to prove—

At Gloria's first hysterical scream, Sue got up automatically. The nurse in her honestly wondered if this was a spell of some sort, if Gloria needed help.

"He can't do this!" Gloria shouted wildly, rushing toward Marv, shaking hands stretched out toward the legal paper as if she intended to tear the will to shreds. "I'll break that will if it's the last thing I ever do."

Marv glanced up, pretending mild surprise. "What's the problem, Gloria? A birth certificate is easy to get these days. One has to be on file. It's the law."

"You hypocrite!" Now her blazing eyes, her frenzied words, were directed straight at Marv. "You're responsible for—for—" Words seemed to fail her.

"Responsible for what, dear?" His tone was mild, faintly puzzled.

"For this lousy, underhanded trick."

"What trick?" asked Marv, pointing out that an investigation of Bobby's birth was a thoroughly legal approach. "It's just to prove that the boy is who you say he is. What's wrong with that?"

At this point Mr. Kim leaped out of Bobby's arms and made a flying tackle for Gloria's ankle. No doubt the jeweled sandals fascinated him. As he began to claw at one sparkling, tempting foot, Gloria gave him a vicious kick.

The kick brought Bobby into screaming action. On his feet, he yelled: "Don't you kick my cat, you liar, you."

Instantly Gloria's hands were savagely on the boy. Before anyone could stop her, she had him backed against one wall. Holding him with one hand, she slapped him with the other again and again until he started to sob. Then, completely berserk, she kicked him hard in the side, and the crystal ball fell from his bulging pocket just as Marv grabbed her arms from behind.

He pulled her away from the boy, who was sobbing, tears streaming from his eyes as he muttered, "I'll get even with you."

Sue went to him, trying to calm him down. "It's all right, honey. Everything is all right. Your mother is upset. She just lost her head for a minute."

Bobby wrenched away from her comforting arm and ran to back himself against the door. "She ain't my mother," he shouted. "I'll tell you who she is."

Gloria pulled away from Marv's restraining hands in a fresh outburst of furious, feverish energy. She was holding fast to the crystal ball as her blazing eyes nailed the boy, who glared back at her. His tear-wet eyes held both terror and desperation.

Martha spoke quietly. "Gloria, do try to get hold of yourself."

Gloria was not to be diverted by calming, warning words, or by the faint whisper of reason in her own mind. She was lost to reason, lost even to sanity as she shrilled in hysterical rage: "I warned you I'd kill you if you ever dared to squeal. Didn't I warn you?"

Then her hand lifted. With all of the strength born of her fury, born of the unbearable frustration of seeing a fortune slip out of her hands, she hurled the crystal ball straight at the boy she had claimed was her son.

It hit Bobby in the temple, a vicious blow which knocked him senseless. The boy did not cry out. The impact was too sudden, too shattering. Bobby simply crumpled to the floor, seemingly lifeless, the blood from the brutal wound seeping down his cheek, and reddening the thick green carpet which covered the library floor.

While Sue and Martha went to the boy, Marv picked up the extension phone. "This makes it a police matter," he said. Then he hesitated, calling to Gloria: "Where do you think you're going?"

Her only reply was a high, shrill laugh as she ran screaming from the room, out of the house, onto the highway.

Hours later she was still struggling along the highway in the darkness of the night. But she was no longer running. She was too spent, too lost in the maze of her disorganized thoughts, to run. Why should she run? What was she running from?

She had no idea. That was what she told the officer when the highway patrol car finally caught up with her. She did not know who she was, where she had come from, where she was going.

When the young officer took her arm gently, asking the questions which needed answering, Gloria stared at him blankly. Then she screamed and screamed and screamed.

Chapter 19

"She said she'd kill me if I didn't do like she said," Bobby explained.

He was lying on the bed in the hospital where for three days he had been in a coma. No one had been permitted in his room except the day nurse and Sue, who had served as his night nurse.

By now, the late afternoon of the fifth day, Sue felt ready to collapse from sheer weariness. But Bobby was going to make it. There was no concussion; the swelling was beginning to go down; and the recuperative powers of youth had taken hold.

When Marv came into the room, Bobby's eyes brightened. Right away he wanted to know: "How is Mr. Kim?"

"He says for you to hurry up and get well," said Marv, drawing up a chair. "He wants somebody to talk to."

Bobby giggled.

Then he sobered as Marv explained that this first visit must be very short. Doctor's orders. "Now we want to know what you meant when you said Gloria was not your mother."

Sue said: "Easy now, Marv. Maybe he doesn't

feel strong enough yet to talk about it."

"I do too feel strong enough," Bobby announced. He wanted to tell all about it.

"Be a good thing for him to get the story off his chest," Marv told Sue, observing that youngsters were like grown-ups. If they had a big worry on their minds, the sooner they talked it out with some understanding person, the sooner they'd get well.

"Go ahead, Bobby," Marv said. "Shoot."

Bobby talked.

It all boiled down to the fact that Bobby's father had been a war hero who had been killed and awarded a posthumous medal for outstanding bravery. Bobby had never seen him, and he could barely remember his mother, who had been killed in a car crash when the boy was three years old.

"Then you weren't making up those stories," Sue interjected, astonished, "about seeing your mummy and daddy in the crystal ball."

Bobby gave her a somewhat patronizing glance. "I was trying to tell you the truth. You wouldn't listen."

The perpetual cry of youth, Sue thought, feeling guilty of what suddenly seemed stupidity.

An aunt had taken care of him for a year, Bobby went on. She was real nice. She was the one who had told him all about his beautiful mummy and his brave, handsome daddy. But then she had gotten married to somebody or other, and she had gone off to some far away country and left him in the charge of Old Lady Thompson.

Sue interrupted with another question: "You mean the lady who ran this home for problem children?"

No. Nothing like that.

At points, Bobby's account was a little garbled. What they gathered was that Mrs. Thompson was an elderly woman of limited means who lived in a big frame house on one of the shabby streets in Hollywood. She added to her income by taking in foster children.

She wasn't too bad, Bobby said. Only she never gave them enough to eat, and she was a little cracked. Bobby figured she was cracked because she was forever bragging how she had once been an actress in the silent movies. Which was pretty silly. How could that ugly old crow who went around with straggly hair, wearing floppy bedroom slippers, ever have been an actress?

Sue's reprimand was gentle. "Just because she was old and no longer pretty, honey, you shouldn't call her an old crow."

Marv grinned.

"Well," said Bobby, "that was what her nephew called her." Behind her back, that is.

"You mean," Marv prodded, "Mrs. Thompson had a nephew living with her?"

Bill Duggan, his name was, Bobby explained. And no, he didn't exactly live there. He was an agent for some show people. Sometimes he'd come around and borrow money from his aunt. She was always good for a touch where this nephew was concerned. Only one time, about six months ago, she was real short of cash. So she asked Bill when he was going to pay back a little of what he owed her. And Bill said he figured I might go over big on TV. So maybe he could pay her back by getting me on a commercial.

"And that's how I got to be a TV actor," Bobby said.

"Bobby!" exclaimed Sue, finding this hard to believe. "Are you saying you were on TV? You aren't just making this up?"

"Stop interrupting," Marv frowned, then laughed when Bobby echoed his words.

"Yeah. Stop interrupting me. I'm a very sick boy, and how can I tell you all I got to tell you if you keep asking if I'm telling the truth?"

"I'm sorry, darling," Sue said, looking disconcerted.

Of course he was on this silly old TV commercial. What he had to do was take a bite of some silly old bread called Yummy Yummy bread. Then he had to show all his teeth and say how good it tasted. Only it tasted awful.

"Never mind about the bread, kid. How does Gloria get into the story?" Glancing at his watch, Marv saw they were racing against time. The doctor had allowed them thirty minutes.

That was where she got acquainted with him, Bobby explained. She had been working on a TV commercial in another studio. One day she stopped him in the hall and said she had heard he was a little genius as an actor.

"Only I wasn't no genius," Bobby interrupted himself to explain. And he didn't want to be an actor. What he wanted when he grew up was to be a cop and go out and catch criminals.

"A laudable ambition," Marv approved. But first things first. "You met Gloria in the hall, and she went out of her way to show you. Then what?"

Then, said Bobby, a long time later, just a few weeks ago, Gloria came to the house with this agent guy who was Mrs. Thompson's nephew. It turned out, Bill Duggan was Gloria's agent, too. And they all went into a huddle in Old Lady Thompson's kitchen. "And they told me they had a little outside job for me to do."

It was an acting job, but not before the TV cameras; a different kind of job. He was to let Gloria take him to this wealthy home where there was a real sick guy who was about to die. And it would do him a lot of good, they said, if he believed he had a little boy he had never seen. "So I was to pretend I was this guy's little boy."

He hadn't wanted to, Bobby declared, and suddenly there were tears in his eyes. He didn't want to pretend he was somebody he wasn't, to fool some poor fellow who was real sick. It didn't seem right. But they kept saying he was such a wonderful little actor, he could get away with it. And after Bill Duggan promised his aunt a lot of money if she'd put on the pressure—"she threatened to send me off to an orphanage if I didn't do like I was told."

Then later, after it was all set up—"That Gloria got me alone and swore she'd kill me if I ever told the real truth to anybody."

It was not what Sue would have termed an easy story to believe—until later.

Later, they sat in a little restaurant, and Marv sipped a cocktail and lit two cigarettes, both of which he forgot to smoke, while he told her about the information he had in his files concerning Gloria.

This included the fact that once upon a time, at age fourteen, she had been sent to a mental institution, after a murderous attack on the old lady from whom she had stolen a few dollars.

Sue shook her head, not in disbelief, but in a kind of shock. "It's almost unbelievable, Marv, what some people will do because of money."

"Not because of money," he corrected her. "It's because of the love of money. That makes it like any other obsession. It becomes a compulsion over which the victim has no control. Given enough rein, the person becomes a sick person on the road to insanity, with no return ticket."

They talked for a few moments about the mental institution where Gloria had been taken. According to the last word he had, Marv said, she had had to be confined to a strait jacket.

Sue shuddered. She had served a few months in a mental place for the criminally insane. She knew only too well the shrieking sounds, the taste of fear in her own mouth when she had to approach those unfortunate, demented creatures who had to be physically restrained for the protection of themselves as well as others.

"And I imagined you were in love with her," Sue said, studying the beautiful broiled steak which the waitress set in front of her. Marv had insisted on ordering a real dinner, not the toast and tea which was all she could possibly eat. Now, to her vast surprise, she discovered that she was ravenous.

Suddenly she felt relaxed, all tension gone, as she listened to Marv explain the reason he had pretended to play up to Gloria.

"She took a fancy to my ugly mug," he said ruefully, "or so she claimed."

Sue cut in sweetly, "It's your fascinating personality, Marv. It's much more deadly than a Hollywood profile."

"Very true." He grinned, lit a fresh cigarette to smoke with his coffee, and went on: "Well, I had to give her a bit of encouragement in her romantic ideas if I was to prevent her from bringing in an outside lawyer to write Dave's will."

"I see." What Sue did not see was why she had not understood all this without being told.

Why had she been so quick to judge Marv, to suspect him of double-dealing that was completely out of character? Was it some strange female quirk, she wondered, always to suspect the worst of the man she liked the best?

"One thing worries me," she said, astonished as

she found herself unable to resist a wedge of luscious, juicy blackberry pie.

"What's that, honey?" The endearing word slipped out casually, and Sue experienced a slight heart palpitation.

"Bobby. What will happen to the boy now?" It would never do to send him back to Mrs. Thompson. They couldn't set him adrift, either.

"I've been giving him a lot of thought," Marv said, beckoning the waitress to bring some hot coffee. "I am considering adopting him. How's that for an idea?"

"You? Adopt Bobby?"

It was such a surprising suggestion. "It takes a lot of money to raise a child these days," she reminded him. "And since you're just getting a fair start in his law practice, you'd need plenty put aside for his education later on."

Money, he said rather grandly, was no problem at all. Had he neglected to bring her up to date as to the final clause in Dave's will? "With Gloria out of the picture, the major part of what he left comes to his half-brother: namely, me."

"Oh, how wonderful of him," said Sue softly, loving Dave for his generosity, loving the memories she would always cherish of her teen-aged sweetheart.

"The real problem—" and his voice held a deep, urgent worry—"is that the kid needs a mother."

"That's very true, Marv."

"So what do I do about that?"

Carefully avoiding his eyes, Sue said: "Why ask me?"

"Well, you're a very smart gal. I thought you might have a suggestion worthy of consideration."

She shook her head, still refusing to meet his eyes, which were fixed on her suddenly flushed face. She said rather primly, "If you're asking me for advice, I'm sorry. I make it a rule never to give advice about matters that don't concern me."

"But what if this does concern you, dear?"

"How could it?"

"You like the kid, don't you?"

"Like Bobby?" Of course she did, she asserted, lighting a cigarette she did not want, solely to have something to do with her hands, which felt suddenly shaky. She felt shaky all over.

Bobby, she agreed, was an adorable boy in ever so many ways. Actually, she had learned to love his scowling, defiant little face. He was exceptionally bright, too. With the right background and training, she hadn't a doubt but that Bobby would develop into a fine man, would make his mark in the world.

"I'm going to miss him." And then she burst out impulsively: "It would be great to have him to love and care for and help his potentialities develop."

"Fine!" Marv exclaimed. "That's certainly a relief off of my mind, having it all settled. Now you and I can get married and move into the big house with Mother. She loves the kid, too. So she'll be delighted to baby-sit when you and I want to go out for an evening on the town."

Her lips soundlessly sought for words.

Then he reached for her hand, and when she felt his warm, urgent touch she looked up at last. He was leaning toward her, his eyes ablaze with the deep, unutterable longing of a man looking at the one girl he had ever truly loved.

"I love you, Sue." He took both of her hands. "I always have. You know that, don't you?"

When she was silent, inwardly fighting the curious acrobatics of her heart, he went on: "The last time I told you how I felt, you said it was wrong for us to love each other."

"I said," she reminded him in a whisper, "that it would be wrong to hurt Dave."

"Yes. But Dave is now beyond hurting, and there is nothing, no one to stand between us. Why are you afraid to look at me, Sue?"

"I'm not."

"You are." He said, very surely, "A man knows when a girl loves him but is afraid to say so. I think that's your trouble, my darling. Am I right?"

"Maybe," she said faintly, at last forcing herself to meet his eyes. Suddenly tears squeezed from beneath her lashes, although she couldn't imagine why.

Why should a girl cry when an intolerably lovely miracle was happening to her?

"Listen," he said, leaning toward her, crushing her hot, trembling hands in his.

"Right outside there is a guard railing. Beyond

the railing there are some cement steps, about twenty of them. Do you know where they lead?"

"Where?"

"Right down to a stretch of beach which I've never forgotten. I'll bet you haven't forgotten, either."

Her heart gave a furious lurch.

"And it just so happens there is a moon tonight, like on that other night. Remember?"

Wordlessly she nodded.

"So all we have to do is go down the steps; start walking along the beach in the moonlight, and there we'll be—all ready to take up where we left off all those long, long years ago. How does that sound?"

At long last she found her voice. "It sounds wonderful." And with the words she gave him a smile. Her eyes, fixed in his, gave him her heart for tonight and for all the tomorrows to come.

"We'd better hurry," she said as he draped her coat over her shoulders, "before the moon goes under a cloud the way it did that other time."

Marv took her arm and squeezed it hard. "This night was worth waiting for," he murmured.